Mee

Alex — quiet lad from ... the team in survival skil... and Alex is determined to follow in his footsteps, whatever it takes. He who dares . . .

Li – Expert in martial arts and free-climbing, Li can g to grips with most situations . . .

P o – The laid-back Argentinian is a mechanical g   s, and with his medical skills he can patch up in ies as well as motors . . .

**H   ** – An ace hacker, Hex is first rate at code-b king and can bypass most security systems . . .

A ber – Her top navigational skills mean the team ar rarely lost. Rarely lost for words either, rich-girl Ar ber can show some serious attitude . . .

With plenty of hard work and training, together th are Alpha Force – an elite squad of young pe ple dedicated to combating injustice throughout th world.

In *Rat-Catcher* Alpha Force are in South America, on th trail of a dangerous drugs baron . . .

w w.kidsatrandomhouse.co.uk/alphaforce

Also available in the Alpha Force series:

SURVIVAL
DESERT PURSUIT
HOSTAGE
RED CENTRE

Coming soon:

HUNTED

chris ryan

ALPHA FORCE

RAT-CATCHER

RED
FOX

ALPHA FORCE: RAT-CATCHER
A RED FOX BOOK 0 09 943925 5

First published in Great Britain by Red Fox,
an imprint of Random House Children's Books, 2002

This edition published 2004

5 7 9 10 8 6 4

Papers used by Random House Children's Books are natural, recyclable
products made from wood grown in sustainable forests. The manufacturing
processes conform to the environmental regulations of the country of origin.

Typeset in Sabon by Palimpsest Book Production Limited,
Polmont, Stirlingshire

Red Fox Books are published by Random House Children's Books,
61–63 Uxbridge Road, London W5 5SA,
a division of The Random House Group Ltd,
in Australia by Random House Australia (Pty) Ltd,
20 Alfred Street, Milsons Point, Sydney, NSW 2061, Australia,
in New Zealand by Random House New Zealand Ltd,
18 Poland Road, Glenfield, Auckland 10, New Zealand,
and in South Africa by Random House (Pty) Ltd,
Endulini, 5A Jubilee Road, Parktown 2193, South Africa

THE RANDOM HOUSE GROUP Limited Reg. No. 954009
www.kidsatrandomhouse.co.uk

A CIP catalogue record for this book is available from the British Library.

Printed and bound in Great Britain by
Cox & Wyman Ltd, Reading, Berkshire

Author photograph © Colin Thomas
Cover image, Getty Images by the Image Bank

ALPHA FORCE

The field of
operation...

CARIBBEAN
SEA

VENEZUELA

COLOMBIA

ECUADOR   SOUTH
           AMERICA

PERU   BRAZIL

ONE

Quito, the capital city of Ecuador . . .

The sleek, black 4x4 slipped into the Old Town area and prowled through the narrow, cobbled streets like a panther. The windows were fitted with mirrored glass to protect the driver from curious eyes, but no-one noticed the big car as it whispered past. It was Easter in Quito, which meant it was *Carnaval* time and, although it was after midnight, the streets were full of wet, happy people chucking water bombs at one another. A gang of young people overtook the slow-moving car, pausing only to check their brightly coloured masks and costumes in the mirrored glass before running on in pursuit of a rival gang. The driver barely glanced at them.

He had no interest in *Carnaval*.

He was out hunting.

A row of five high-powered halogen lamps were bracketed to the roof of the 4x4. The three central lamps faced forwards over the bonnet but the two end lamps were angled so that they pointed off to each side. The driver brought the car to a stop across the entrance to a dark alleyway. He opened a compartment in the dashboard and took out a dull, black, snub-nosed pistol with a silencer screwed onto the end of the barrel. Placing the pistol on the passenger seat beside him, he switched on the left-side halogen lamp. Instantly, a powerful beam of light flooded into the alleyway and picked out a kissing couple. The startled pair sprang apart, turning their heads away from the blinding light and shielding their eyes with their hands. The driver studied the couple briefly, then turned his attention to the alleyway behind them. It was empty. The driver showed no impatience as he flicked off the halogen lamp and moved on. He was a patient hunter and he knew he would track down his prey before the night was over.

Twenty minutes later, as the driver edged his car out into a small, cobbled square, he found what he was looking for. The young *Carnaval* gang had finally cornered their rivals and a spectacular water fight was under way. A small crowd had gathered in the square to watch the fun and a thin, dark-haired boy of about thirteen was hovering at the back, directly behind a pair of American tourists. The boy was the only one not craning his neck to see the water fight.

The driver narrowed his eyes as he caught sight of the boy. He killed the 4x4's headlights and eased the big car back into the shadows. The boy edged closer to the American tourists, then glanced quickly from left to right to make sure no-one was watching him. As the boy turned his head, the driver saw the tell-tale red smears around his nose and mouth. It looked as though the boy had been helping himself to a pot of raspberry jam but the driver knew differently. The red marks were a rash caused by sniffing glue.

The driver's mouth tightened. The boy was

definitely one of Quito's street kids. Street *rats*, he preferred to call them. There were thousands of them infesting his beautiful city, begging, stealing and making their filthy nests in back alleys. As far as he was concerned, they were vermin and every one he exterminated made the streets of Quito that little bit cleaner. They were street rats – and he was the Rat-catcher.

The boy stepped up behind one of the tourists and took out a razor blade. The tourist had left a fat wallet sticking out of the back pocket of his jeans. With an expert flick of his razor, the boy slit the pocket and let the wallet fall onto his outstretched hand. He made the wallet disappear into his jacket as he sauntered out of the square without looking back. The driver put his car into gear and followed the boy at a distance. When the boy turned down a relatively empty street, the driver flicked on the halogen lamps. The boy twisted round, his dark eyes wide in the glare of the lamps, and the driver smiled. The boy tripped, picked himself up, then set off at a stumbling run with the big car at his heels.

The hunt was on.

In another back alley in a quieter part of the Old Town Eliza was sitting on the wet cobbles with her back against a ventilator grille. Her little brother Toby was fast asleep beside her, curled up inside their father's woollen poncho. The alley was behind a restaurant and the grille was venting hot air from the kitchens. The warm breeze at her back eased her shivering, but the rich smells of cooking were making her stomach rumble. She yawned and looked across at her big brother Marco, who was building their shelter for the night.

'Nearly there,' said Marco, giving her a cheerful smile as he arranged the sheets of cardboard against the back wall of the restaurant, making a sloping roof over the floor of wooden pallets.

Eliza nodded, then yawned again. She pulled her legs up to her empty belly and rested her head on her knees for a moment. Her eyes began to close but she jerked herself awake. Her little brother Toby was only two, so it was all right for him to be asleep, but she was six and that was too old to be carried to bed. Eliza sat up straighter and waited for Marco to finish the shelter.

'You know,' said Marco, 'I think Oscar left this wood and cardboard out here on purpose, just for us. And he promised us a plateful of leftovers when the restaurant closes.'

'Because you cleaned his shoes for free until they shone like mirrors,' said Eliza.

'Only to repay his kindnesses,' said Marco. 'Anyway, that's not why Oscar helps us.'

'Why, then?'

'I think he helps us because he loves your beautiful smile, little Eliza.'

Eliza beamed. She liked Oscar too. He was the owner of the restaurant and he had been helping them out in little ways ever since their mother . . .

Eliza's smile fell away as she remembered. It was hard to believe that a few short months ago her family had celebrated Christmas together in their own house. So many bad things had happened to them since the New Year, when her father had gone up into the higher mountain passes to look for a lost ewe. He had not come home that night. The next day a search party discovered his dead body at the bottom of a ravine. Two weeks later the family had been forced to leave their small farm on the lower slopes of the Andes to make way for a new tenant.

Eliza's father was a gentle, intelligent, hard-working man who loved his family. He was also a Quechua Indian. Quechuas were an old race who had been natives of Ecuador long before the Spaniards invaded. In modern-day Ecuador they were often treated as second-class citizens. Eliza's mother came from a wealthy white family and they had disowned her when she married him. After he died, Eliza's mother had swallowed her pride and returned to Quito with her children to ask for help. Her family had refused to see them. The problem was that Eliza, Marco and Toby were *mestizos*, or mixed-race children. To make matters worse, while Toby had his mother's pale skin and fair hair, Eliza and Marco were both *morenos,* meaning their skin was dark.

For three months their mother had struggled on, hoping the family would have a change of heart and help her and the children. They never did. Finally, worn out after months of struggling to get by, she had come down with severe food-poisoning and died overnight.

Eliza blinked fiercely in the dark alleyway, squashing away the tears that were trying to form in her eyes as she thought about her mother. She bent over her little brother, brushing his blond curls away from his face and tucking the poncho more firmly under his chin.

'Your room is ready now, madam,' said Marco, with an elaborate bow.

Eliza gave him a wobbly smile, then crawled inside the cardboard lean-to. Marco's precious shoe-shine kit, their only means of earning a living, was already in the shelter and Eliza settled down with her back resting against the wooden box.

'Comfy?' asked Marco.

Eliza nodded and held out her arms. Marco gently picked up Toby and handed him to her.

'Here, you can add these to the savings,' said Marco, handing over the coins they had earned from another long day on their shoe-shine corner. 'Soon we will have enough to rent a room,' he continued, as Eliza tucked the coins into the drawstring purse tied around her neck. 'In the meantime, at least we are together. We will be fine here.'

'Are you sure?' whispered Eliza.

Marco reached out, lifted Eliza's chin and looked into her eyes. 'Yes,' he said firmly. 'I can look after you. I am thirteen now. Nearly a man. You will be safe with me, Eliza. I promise.'

Eliza stared into Marco's warm brown eyes and suddenly the flimsy cardboard shelter felt as safe as a fortress. Her beaming smile returned and Marco grinned back at her.

Then the silence was disturbed by stumbling footsteps at the other end of the alleyway.

'Quiet as a mouse!' warned Marco, before hastily pulling a sheet of cardboard over the entrance to the lean-to. Through a narrow gap in the cardboard sheets, Eliza saw Marco check the shelter briefly, then give a nod of satisfaction. With the doorway covered, it looked to be nothing more than a stack of cardboard waiting for the refuse-collectors.

The footsteps were getting closer. Marco turned and stood with his feet apart and his fists clenched, ready to defend his family. As she stared through the gap in the cardboard walls, Eliza felt her spine stiffen with anxiety. Then a figure stumbled into the dim pool of light coming from the restaurant kitchens. Eliza relaxed. It was only another boy, the same age and height as Marco. He was thin and dirty, with a red, glue-sniffer's rash around his mouth, and he looked exhausted.

'Are you all right?' asked Marco.

The boy ignored him. Instead, he looked around the alleyway and groaned when he realized it was a dead end. He glanced back over his shoulder, then fumbled an expensive-looking leather wallet out of his jacket. He pulled out a wad of notes, threw the wallet to the ground and stuffed the money into his trouser pocket.

'Did you steal that?' asked Marco. 'You shouldn't steal.'

The boy gave a gasping laugh, then checked the dark entrance to the alleyway again. 'You haven't been on the streets long, have you?'

'A few weeks,' said Marco. 'My name is Marco.'

'Leopoldo,' grunted the boy. 'But everyone calls me Leo. Listen, Marco, perhaps we can help one another out.'

'How?' asked Marco.

'Have you heard of the Rat-catcher?' said Leo.

Eliza shuddered in the lean-to. Everyone knew about the man in the black car who hunted them down like rats. He was an evil legend amongst the street kids. Nobody knew what he looked like – and nobody wanted to. If you saw his face, you were as good as dead.

'I've heard of him,' said Marco.

'Yeah, well, he's after me,' said Leo.

'What! Right now?' asked Marco.

'He's clever,' said Leo. 'I've only just realized what he's been doing. I thought I was getting away from him, but he's been herding me. Edging me here, into the quiet part of town.'

Leo shivered and looked over his shoulder again as he remembered how he had run through the grids of narrow streets, twisting and turning to get away from the big car. Every time he had stopped to catch his breath, the black bonnet had nosed into view at the top of the street and the halogen lamps had picked him out of the darkness once more.

'Perhaps you've lost him now,' said Marco.

As though in answer, they all heard the growing

hum of engine noise as the big car idled into the street at the end of the alleyway. In the shelter, Eliza clutched the sleeping Toby more tightly and bit her lip to stop herself from crying out.

'So,' said Leo hastily, glancing at the high wall to his left, then back to Marco, 'if you help me out now, I'll help you out later. I'll show you how to survive on the streets. Teach you some of the rules. Deal?'

There was no time for hesitation. The darkness at the entrance to the alleyway was growing paler by the second. Marco turned his back on Leo as though he was thinking. He looked straight at the shelter and put a finger to his lips. Eliza understood that he was telling her to stay still and quiet. It was their only chance.

'Deal,' said Marco, turning back to Leo.

Leo smiled. 'OK. You help me onto the top of that wall, then I'll pull you up after me. That way we can both get out of here.'

Marco nodded, then ran to the wall and braced himself against it, making a human ladder for Leo to climb. Leo reached the top of the wall just as the big car turned the corner into the alleyway. Suddenly the whole area was lit up as bright as day. The car moved slowly closer as Marco held his hand up to Leo, waiting for him to grasp it.

Leo hesitated, then looked down at Marco. 'Street rule number one,' he said. 'Trust no-one.'

'Wait!' said Marco, but Leo had already disappeared. Marco tried to scrabble his way up the smooth, whitewashed stone, but the wall was too high. He dropped to the ground again and stood with his back against the wall as a car door slammed shut and the Rat-catcher stepped in front of the 4x4. The blinding light of the lamps turned him into a black silhouette.

'It wasn't me,' said Marco, shielding his eyes against the glare as the man kicked the discarded wallet across the cobblestones towards him.

'Doesn't matter,' said the Rat-catcher. 'You're all the same. Thieving little rats. You'll do.'

He brought his hand up and levelled the pistol at Marco. In the lean-to, Eliza felt her breath stop in her throat. She closed her eyes and clamped a hand over her mouth as she heard Marco give a scared, hopeless whimper. There was one muffled crack, then a dull thud as her brother's body fell to the cobbles.

Eliza opened her eyes again and saw that the white-washed wall was splashed with glistening red blood. She sat in the little shelter, frozen with shock as the Rat-catcher grabbed Marco by his ankles and dragged him towards the boot of the car. A noise from the kitchens made the man turn and Eliza saw the face of the Rat-catcher for the first time. She stared at him until every detail was etched into her memory.

The Rat-catcher returned to the task of dragging Marco to the boot of his car. As her brother's body began to disappear into the darkness behind the halogen lamps, Eliza made herself take one last look at his face. His head was tilted back and his brown eyes were open in a wide, blank stare. A few moments ago those eyes had been full of warmth as Marco smiled at her. Now all the warmth was gone.

The black car slowly backed out of the alley and roared off, leaving Eliza sitting in the sudden dark. The air made a harsh noise in her throat as, finally, she took a breath. Marco, her protector, was gone. Eliza thought she would never, ever feel safe again.

TWO

The Nevada desert, eight months later . . .

Amber lay flat on her belly and ducked her head behind the scant cover of a yucca plant as the searchlight cut through the darkness. She was lying on the outer limit of the beam's range, but still she felt terribly exposed as the wedge of light swept across the desert towards her. Amber pressed her cheek against the stony ground and a shiver ran through her as the cold bit into her bones. It was six degrees below zero now, but when the helicopter had touched down in the desert earlier that afternoon, she and the other four members of Alpha Force had stepped out into blazing sunshine and temperatures in the high twenties. The Nevada desert in December was a place of extremes.

The edge of the searchlight beam reached her hiding-place, grazing the yucca plant and giving each spiky leaf a temporary shadow. As soon as the beam moved on, Amber checked the luminous dial on her stopwatch. Ninety seconds. Surely that was far too short? She bit her lip, then put the thought out of her head and got on with the business at hand. First, she cocked her head and listened. A hunting owl hooted close by, but otherwise the desert was quiet. Cautiously, Amber raised her head and peered through the yucca leaves. The searchlight beam had temporarily destroyed her natural night vision, so she reached up and pulled her night-vision goggles down over her eyes. The searchlight tower was inside a compound, which lay ahead of her across a flat expanse of pebbly, red ground. Amber activated the goggles and the compound appeared in her sights, bathed in a weird green light. It was a cluster of low, prefabricated buildings, protected by a steel-mesh boundary fence. The fence rose twice as high as a man and it was topped with coils of razor wire. It ran in an unbroken line all round the back of the complex.

Amber stared at the fence, trying to see whether it was electrified. She raised her head above the yucca plant to get a better look and, as she did so, a German Shepherd dog started barking fiercely. Amber slammed back down onto the sand, cursing herself for being so careless. She had been lying behind the yucca bush for twenty minutes, timing the searchlight sweeps and the dog patrols with her stopwatch. She should have known that it was time for the guard and his dog to appear at the rear of the complex again. How could she have been so stupid?

The guard walked towards the fence with the barking dog straining on its lead ahead of him. Amber flattened herself against the ground. She was dressed all in black so she was sure the guard could not see her in the darkness beyond the compound, but something had alerted the dog. The breeze was still blowing her way, so she knew the animal could not have picked up her scent. Did dogs have sharper eyes than people? Had it spotted the movement when she raised her head above the yucca bush? Or maybe the lenses of her night-vision goggles had reflected a glimmer of light?

The guard and the dog had reached the boundary fence. The dog threw itself against the steel mesh, which answered one question for her. The fence was not electrified. The guard switched on a powerful torch and sent the beam zigzagging through the darkness. The beam hit the yucca bush and the dog's barking rose to a crescendo. Amber groaned inwardly. She had blown it. She tensed, preparing to break cover and run for it. Then the owl she had heard earlier burst from the ground a few metres in front of her. It fluttered in the torch beam for a few seconds, blinded by the light, and the dog went into overdrive. The owl recovered itself and glided away, flying low and silent across the desert. The guard let the beam follow it for a few seconds, then he clicked the torch off, dragged the frantic dog away from the fence and continued on his way.

Amber closed her eyes. She was covered in a cold sweat and felt as though she was about to melt into the desert sand with relief. She gave herself a few seconds to recover, then turned and commando-crawled across the stony ground, heading for the cover of the towering, red sandstone mesa that rose from the desert behind her.

Alex, Li, Hex and Paulo, the other four members of Alpha Force, were waiting for Amber on the other side of the mesa. They jumped when she scurried around the corner of the huge rock and flopped down beside them, sending small stones skittering everywhere. They were all dressed in black too, and they had been applying camouflage cream while they waited for her. In the faint starlight they blended almost perfectly into the shadowed rock face. Amber grinned when she saw their anxious eyes blinking out at her from their blackened faces.

'Hey, guys,' she whispered mock-seriously, pointing to the smears of camouflage cream then making dabbing motions at her own face. 'You have a little something, just here . . .'

'*Dios Mio*, Amber!' hissed Paulo.

'What?' said Amber coolly.

'We thought you'd been caught,' said Li, tucking a wisp of her long black hair behind her ear.

'What, me?' said Amber. 'Nah. No chance.'

'So, don't tell me,' said Hex, folding his arms and raising his eyebrows at her. 'That dog wasn't barking a warning. It was ordering a pizza.'

'An owl spooked it, that's all. Aww. Were you scared, sweetie? I wasn't.'

'Then why are you sweating?' asked Hex.

Amber swiped at her forehead then glared at Hex. 'I – I got a little hot.'

'Amber,' said Li, 'it's below freezing out here.'

'Yeah, well I wasn't scared, OK? I—'

'Amber,' said Alex quietly, 'can we just focus on the job? What did you find out?'

'Oh, OK. There's good news and bad news. First of all, the dog patrols are about five minutes apart.'

'And the good news?' asked Alex.

'That was the good news,' said Amber, suddenly serious. 'The bad news is, the searchlight sweep is repeated every ninety seconds.'

'Ninety seconds?' said Paulo. 'But that is not enough time. We cannot get across the open ground, cut the wire and get into the building in less than ninety seconds. We will be seen. We will be caught . . .'

Paulo trailed to a halt and shared a hopeless look with Li. Alex scowled at the ground and Hex shook his head. Amber watched their reactions and her worst fears were confirmed.

'Hey, come on,' she said. 'We can't give up. A-Watch would've given up, but we're Alpha Force now. We won't give up. Right, guys?'

The others all understood what Amber meant. There was a huge difference between A-Watch and Alpha Force. Six months earlier they had all met for the first time aboard a sail-training ship called the *Phoenix*. The ship was on her maiden voyage, sailing across the Java Sea with a crew of young people from all over the world. The five of them had been put together in A-Watch and had quickly gained the reputation of being the worst watch team in the whole crew. Amber, a black American girl from a family of software billionaires, and Hex, a street-wise Londoner and expert hacker, had taken an instant dislike to one another. Paulo, a handsome Argentinian boy, and Li, a lively Anglo-Chinese girl, had spent their time flirting instead of working. Alex, the fifth member of the team, had withdrawn from the whole messy business, getting on with his work in isolated silence and wishing he was back home in Northumberland.

It had seemed impossible that A-Watch would ever pull together, but when they became castaways on an uninhabited tropical island, they had been forced to start working as a team. In one terrifying week they had survived shark attacks, killer komodo dragons and a group of vicious, modern-day pirates. When Hex had developed blood-poisoning as the result of a deadly komodo bite, Amber had swum through shark-infested waters to reach the medicines that would save him. Now, although they were complete opposites, Amber and Hex were the closest of friends. They all were.

During that life-changing week they had learned a great deal about working together as a team – and Amber had also discovered that the death of her parents in a plane crash a year earlier had not been an accident. The plane had been deliberately sabotaged. At first Amber could not understand why anyone would want to do such a thing, but then she had learned that her parents were much more than they seemed. They had been secretly involved in dangerous undercover work, using some of their vast fortune to help other people. As private individuals, they could go into places where governments and officials were denied access. They could get food and medicines in or smuggle video evidence out. Much of their covert filming had ended up on the international news, forcing governments and authorities into action. The more Amber discovered, the more she understood why her parents had been killed.

Amber had persuaded her uncle to let the five of them carry on the work of her parents and Hex had come up with a name for the team: Alpha Force. 'Alpha' was made up of the initial letters of all their names. It was also the beginning of the Greek alphabet. That was what Alpha Force was supposed to be – a new beginning, coming out of the sacrifice Amber's parents had made.

'Guys?' repeated Amber now, with a touch of desperation in her voice. 'We won't give up on our first real challenge, will we?'

'No way,' said Li. 'We've worked too hard for this.'

They all nodded in agreement as they thought about the past six months. They had spent every school break together, undergoing hard physical and mental training to prepare them for the work ahead. During the school terms, when they went their separate ways, they had each devoted every spare minute to improving their individual talents. Li had worked hard on her martial arts and free climbing. Alex had spent days and nights out on the Northumbrian moors, sharpening his survival skills. Hex was already an expert hacker and code-breaker, but he had made it his business to learn as much as he could about surveillance and security equipment. To the surprise of teachers at her exclusive boarding school in Boston, Amber had become their most dedicated foreign languages student, spending hours every evening in the language lab. She had also forced herself to go sailing in the little family yacht, which had not left the marina since her parents died, so that she could practise her map-reading and navigation. Back home in Argentina, Paulo had taken out motor-bikes, quads and four-wheel-drive vehicles, churning up the dirt tracks that crisscrossed his family cattle ranch until he had perfected his off-road driving skills. He had also put together his own compact tool-kit and carried it with him everywhere in a leather pouch attached to his belt.

'Come on,' said Alex, gazing out at the dark Nevada desert. 'We've got this far. We can't give up now. Let's get thinking. It's going to take us at least four minutes to cover that stretch of open ground, cut through the compound fence and get into the building. Four minutes. But the searchlight sweep comes round every ninety seconds. Any ideas?'

The silence dragged on as everybody racked their brains. As the hope slowly drained out of her, Amber felt the cold of the desert seeping into her bones. She reached for one of the desert camouflage sheets they had sheltered under as they waited for darkness and, with a shaky sigh, wrapped it around her shoulders. Hex watched her absently, then his eyes lit up with excitement.

'That's it!' he whispered. 'I've got it!'

Amber grinned and stood up straighter. 'Knew you'd solve it, puzzle boy,' she crowed. 'What's the plan?'

THREE

As soon as the guard and his dog disappeared round the far corner of the complex, five dark shapes left the cover of the sandstone mesa and ran across the open ground with their heads low, dodging sage brush and yucca plants and leaping over small boulders. They were heading for the compound fence, racing the searchlight beam. Li had tucked all her long, silky hair away under a woollen hat and even dark-skinned Amber was wearing camouflage cream to block any shine from her nose and cheekbones, so only the whites of their eyes reflected the wedge of light as it swept towards them.

They raced on towards the fence, but the searchlight was faster. It flowed across the rough ground towards them with an easy speed. Alex judged the distance to the fence and realized that they were not going to make it. In five seconds they would be floodlit. Four seconds. Three . . .

Alex gave the signal and they all flung themselves to the ground, shaking out the rolled-up camouflage sheets they held in their hands as they went down. When the searchlight beam rolled over them two seconds later, it found nothing but five shallow mounds of desert ground. They waited under the camouflage sheets, keeping their eyes closed against the searchlight beam to preserve their night vision.

As soon as the beam left them, they were up again, bundling up the camouflage sheets as they ran. Seconds later, they reached the fence. Alex knelt and got to work with a powerful pair of bolt-cutters, which snipped through the steel mesh of the fence as though it was tinfoil. He nodded to Paulo and they hooked their fingers through the mesh on each side of the breach. Slowly they bent back the two sections until there was a gap big enough to squeeze through.

One by one, they went down on their bellies and squirmed under the fence. Alex was the last and, as he began to ease through, the searchlight beam was approaching again, sweeping across the compound from the other direction. Amber looked at the searchlight, then down at her stopwatch.

'Fifteen seconds,' she whispered.

Alex wriggled his broad shoulders through the gap, then jerked to a halt halfway under the fence.

'Come on!' hissed Li.

'Can't,' grunted Alex. 'Stuck.'

Li flung herself to the ground next to Alex as the other three ran for cover. They were aiming for a door which was set in the end wall of a long, narrow building. The end wall faced away from the searchlight tower, which meant that there was a small area in front of the door where the searchlight could not penetrate. They reached the door and flattened themselves against the wall on either side of it.

'Ten seconds,' squeaked Amber.

At the fence Li felt along the back of Alex's belt until she found the hook of steel that had snagged him. She grabbed the steel with fingers that had been strengthened by years of free climbing and bent the hook back on itself. As soon as he was free, Alex surged under the gap.

'Go!' he hissed to Li.

She ran to join the others while he stooped and grabbed the fence on each side of the gap. His whole body trembled as he strained to pull the two curls of steel mesh back into line. Slowly they came together as the searchlight raced towards him.

'Now, Alex!' hissed Amber from the shadows.

Alex gave the fence a last, quick survey. The breach was hardly visible, even in the growing light of the approaching searchlight. With luck, the guard would walk right past it.

'Alex!'

Alex let go of the fence and flung himself towards the others, but he was too late. The searchlight reached him and lit him up as though he was on a stage. With one desperate leap, Alex launched himself out of the brilliant pool of light and rolled into the shadow of the doorway. For a few seconds they all froze in place, listening. Alex had only been in the full glare of the beam for a split second, but had he been spotted?

No cries of alarm broke the silence of the desert and the searchlight beam continued steadily on its way. 'I think we got away with it,' whispered Alex after a few seconds.

'Yeah, but the dog patrol is going to come round that corner again and walk right into us in . . .' Amber glanced at her stopwatch. 'In less than two minutes.'

The door had no lock. Instead there was a keypad above the handle. The cover of the keypad was held in place with four tiny screws. Paulo reached into the leather pouch at his belt and pulled out an equally small screwdriver. He applied it to the keypad and pressed a button on the handle. The screwdriver let out a thin whine and, in two seconds, the screw fell into his hand. Hex reached into a rucksack he had brought with him and took out a small black box with two wires coming off it. As soon as Paulo eased the cover away from the keypad, Hex went to work, clipping the wires to the innards of the keypad. The digital display on the box flickered as it went through all the possible combinations and selected the correct sequence of numbers. The door unlocked with a click and swung outwards on silent hinges. Paulo busied himself with replacing the cover on the keypad as Hex stared into the dark corridor beyond the doorway.

'Let's go!' hissed Amber impatiently, staring at her stopwatch.

'Wait.' Hex took a small torch from the rucksack and shone it into the corridor. It seemed to be clear, but Hex was suspicious by nature. He moved the beam around the doorframe, then down to the floor. There was a doormat just inside the doorway. Hex frowned. Why would a doormat be necessary in a place where it hardly ever rained? Carefully, he eased up the corner of the mat and shone the torch underneath. Pressure pads. If anyone stood on the mat, the pads would activate an alarm system.

Hex made sure the others had seen the pressure pads, then he eased the mat down again. He reached into his rucksack and took out an aerosol can. It contained pressurized spring water, and was normally used as a way of keeping cool in the dry heat of the desert day. That was not why Hex was using it.

As the fine mist of water spread into the corridor, a thin, red, knee-high beam came into view in the torchlight. It angled from one side of the corridor to the other, just beyond the doormat. 'See that?' he whispered. 'That's an infra-red laser beam. If we break that beam, it'll set off an alarm.'

'We have to get inside!' hissed Amber. 'There's less than a minute left!'

'OK,' said Hex. 'Follow me, one at a time. Go round the mat, then step over the beam. Once you're on the other side of the beam, don't move an inch. There are probably more of them.'

One by one they eased around the mat, then stepped over the beam. Amber was getting frantic. The time was up, according to her stopwatch. She stepped over the beam and squeezed in beside Hex, Li and Paulo.

'Now you, Alex,' she whispered. But Alex did not follow her over the beam. Instead, he stopped in the doorway and pulled a small, limp, furry body from inside his shirt. It was a dead kangaroo rat. He had found it under some sage brush earlier in the day as they hiked across the desert from the helicopter. The little body had stayed warm inside his shirt and it was beginning to smell a bit.

Alex bent and laid the kangaroo rat on the ground just outside the door. As he straightened, he heard the snuffling pant of the German Shepherd getting louder as it trotted the last few metres towards the corner. In a few seconds the dog would turn the corner and see him. Quickly, Alex stepped into the corridor and stood balancing on the narrow strip of floor at the edge of the mat. He reached behind him and pulled the door shut. The lock clicked into place just as the guard dog rounded the corner. Hex turned off his torch and they stood in the dark corridor, listening intently.

Outside, the dog picked up their scent immediately, as Alex had guessed it would. With a yelping bark, the dog turned and headed for the door, dragging the guard after it. The dog slammed into the door with frantic force. Alex jumped at the noise and began to overbalance onto the doormat. For a few seconds he hung over the pressure pads, windmilling his arms. Finally he found his balance again and slumped back against the wall with a relieved sigh.

Outside, the dog was still barking and scrabbling at the door. Suddenly the door handle rattled loudly as the guard tried it. 'What is it, boy?' he said. His voice was so loud, it was as though he was standing in the corridor next to them. 'Hang on a minute. It's only a dead kangaroo rat. Come on, you stupid mutt. Leave it. It's time for my coffee break.'

The dog's frantic barks grew fainter as the guard dragged it away from the door. Inside the corridor, Hex flicked on the torch again. He trained it on a control panel at the other end of the corridor. 'That'll turn off the beams,' he said, turning to Li. 'Think you can make it?'

Li took the aerosol can and sprayed a fine mist ahead of her. The mist revealed a complex cat's cradle of red beams running the length of the short corridor. Paulo groaned when he saw them but Li gave him a cheeky, sideways grin.

'Easy-peasy,' she whispered and Paulo smiled back at her proudly.

Li took a deep breath and set off. She was wearing a skin-tight Lycra bodysuit and her hair was tucked up into a hat to keep it out of the way of the beams. Slowly, Li made her way along the corridor, turning, balancing and bending into near-impossible shapes. At last there were only two beams to go, but they were angled in such a way that it was impossible to step over them. Li stood poised for a moment, judging angles and distances, then she raised her arms above her head and went up onto her toes. She soared into the air and jack-knifed over the first beam. Landing on her hands, she pushed off again, flipped neatly over the second beam and made a perfect landing right in front of the control panel.

With a flourish, Li turned off the laser beams. The others ran to join her as she swung open the door at the end of the corridor. Hex flicked his torch around the dark room on the other side of the door until the beam lit up a high-powered computer. His fingers were already keying the air as he settled into the chair in front of the keyboard. Now it was his turn.

Like all hackers, Hex hated the simple point-and-click operating system most civilians relied on. He did not need a user-friendly mouse to lead him around by the nose. Instead he went in the hacker's way, pounding direct commands out on the keyboard and communicating with the computer in its own language. Within a minute he was into the system and scanning the list of files. He found the file he wanted and tried to open it. The file was password-protected.

Hex backtracked, returning to the list of files and scanning the names. There it was – a file labelled PASSWORDS. Hex grinned and shook his head at the stupidity of most computer-users as he opened the file, retrieved the necessary password and returned to the original file. He opened the file and sat back, smiling. Then the smile slipped from his face as an unreadable mish-mash of characters appeared on the screen.

'Damn,' muttered Hex, frowning at the monitor.

'Problems?' asked Alex.

'It's encrypted.'

'Can you do anything?' asked Li.

'There are a couple of options,' said Hex.

'Well, you'd better get on with it, code-boy,' hissed Amber, looking up from her stopwatch. 'That guard and his dog are due back any minute now.'

Hex frowned at the screen, considering what to do next. The owners of this computer had not scored very highly in the intelligence stakes so far, so he decided to go for the most obvious solution. Sometimes simply copying an encrypted file would be enough to decipher it, because the computer always copied a file in plaintext form, unless it had been told not to. Hex was guessing that this computer had been given no such instruction. His fingers hammered at the keys again as he gave the computer the copy command. Instantly, the mish-mash of characters transformed themselves into a readable sentence.

WELCOME, USER. TO START THE PROGRAM, PRESS ANY KEY.

Hex smiled at the others before leaning forward and hitting the space bar. Another sentence appeared on the screen:

COUNTDOWN SEQUENCE INITIATED — YOU NOW HAVE TWENTY SECONDS TO EVACUATE THE BUILDING.

'What?' Hex jumped to his feet. 'What countdown sequence?' he demanded.

A pleasant female voice emerged from the speakers next to the computer. 'Nineteen . . . eighteen . . .' said the voice mildly, as though it was reading out the weather forecast.

'Whatever it is, we're not staying to find out,' yelled Amber. 'Run!'

FOUR

They raced out of the room and down the corridor, with Paulo in the lead. Too late, he remembered the pressure pads under the mat. Unable to stop, he leaped over the mat instead, slamming into the door beyond. It flew open and crashed against the outside wall. Paulo rolled across the packed dirt of the compound, came up onto his feet again and continued running for the fence, with the others at his heels. They could still hear the computer voice faintly, as it counted down behind them.

'Twelve . . . eleven . . .'

Paulo slid the last metre on his belly, grabbed at the steel mesh of the fence and forced the two sides apart. He scrambled through, then turned and grabbed Li by the hands. With one powerful yank he pulled her through the gap in the fence.

'Eight . . . seven . . . six . . .'

'*Dios Mio*,' gasped Paulo, leaning down to grab hold of Amber.

'Four . . . three . . .'

Hex came through next, then Alex. They scrambled to their feet and were running for the protection of the mesa when the night sky behind them lit up with a series of explosions. They all dived to the ground and lay there with their hands over their heads. The explosions continued but there was no blast, no burning rain of debris falling around them. Alex took his hands away from his head. The explosions sounded vaguely familiar to him. They sounded just like . . .

'Fireworks,' said Alex. 'Are they fireworks?'

Cautiously they raised their heads and peered at the complex, then they sat up and stared in open astonishment. Rockets of all shapes, colours and sizes were shooting up into the night sky, but the centrepiece was a length of metal gridwork which was bracketed to the rooftop. Hundreds of fireworks had been wired to the gridwork and they spelled out a series of words in bright, neon colours.

WELL DONE, ALPHA FORCE. YOU HAVE SUCCESSFULLY COMPLETED THE EXERCISE. MERRY CHRISTMAS!

'Oh, for crying out loud,' groaned Alex, putting a hand over his thumping heart as a tall black man hurried out of one of the buildings and walked over to the fence.

'Hello, Uncle,' said Amber weakly, as John Middleton grinned through the fence at her. 'Very funny. Ha ha.'

John Middleton drove them out through the main gates of the complex and turned onto the highway, heading south to McCarran International Airport on the edge of Las Vegas. Now that Alpha Force had completed the exercise, they were all flying off to different locations for the Christmas break. Hex was going to stay with Amber and her uncle in New York, Li was spending the holiday with Paulo and his family in Argentina, and Alex was flying out to join his father in Ecuador.

John Middleton gave the guards a friendly wave as he passed them and they replied with a salute. Alex noticed that they were wearing American military uniforms. He turned to look at Amber's uncle.

'Did we just break into an actual military base?'

'Only a little one,' smiled John Middleton. 'It's a security facility on the edge of the Nevada Test Site. You know, where they used to test nuclear weapons.'

'Yeah, we caught a glimpse of that as we flew over this afternoon,' said Hex, remembering the lunar landscape of craters and huge pits in the middle of nowhere.

'Are they friends of yours?' asked Li, nodding back at the soldiers.

'Let's just say they owed me one,' said John Middleton. He grinned at Amber. 'They're not too pleased to have been outsmarted by a bunch of kids. And, yes, I admit it – I'm impressed. I had most of my security concentrated at the front of the complex. We thought it was impossible for anyone to creep up on us from behind. There's nothing but hundreds of miles of desert back there. How did you do it?'

Amber smirked. 'We picked the most run-down, hole-in-the-wall helicopter tour company we could find and offered the guy double his normal fee to take us as far into the desert as he could. Then we hiked the rest of the way. I navigated.'

John Middleton shook his head and tutted. 'You mean this pilot dumped a group of kids in the middle of the desert without a second thought? Some people.'

'We were very persuasive,' smiled Paulo.

'So, Uncle,' prompted Amber. 'We passed the final test.'

'Hmm,' was John Middleton's only reply.

'You said when we passed the test, we could go on our first mission. Remember?'

'We'll see,' said John Middleton vaguely.

As soon as John Middleton had left them alone in the airport departure-lounge, Amber turned to the others. 'He's not going to do it,' she said bluntly. 'He's not going to find us a mission.'

'Are you sure?' asked Hex.

'I know my uncle. When he says, "We'll see," like that, it means he's not going to do it. When it comes down to it, he's too scared to send us anywhere that might be dangerous. So listen, here's what we're gonna do. Everyone keep your eyes open over the next few weeks, OK? We're going to have to find our own mission.'

'American Airways flight to Quito now boarding at Gate Three,' announced the loudspeaker system.

'That's me,' said Alex, getting to his feet and grabbing his bags. 'Have a good Christmas, everyone.'

They all shouted their goodbyes as Alex moved off towards the departure-gate.

'And remember,' called Amber over the bobbing heads of the crowd. 'Keep your eyes open!'

Alex collapsed into his seat, pulled his cap down over his eyes and slept away the flight. The man in the next seat shook him awake as the plane began the descent to Quito airport.

'Time to buckle up,' smiled the man. 'And take a peek out there. It's quite a sight.'

Alex looked out through the window of the plane and gasped at the beautiful landscape below him. The plane was flying down the central highland valley which ran from north to south between two chains of craggy, snow-topped Andean peaks. The sun was just rising above the peaks, bathing the mountains and the valley in a golden glow. Quito, the capital of Ecuador, was spread out ahead of them, resting snugly in the bottom of the highland valley. The sun highlighted the red roofs and whitewashed buildings of the Old Town area and, beyond that, it reflected off the surface of the Pan-American Highway, which carried on down the central valley like a long, thin tail.

'It's called the Valley of the Volcanoes,' said Alex's neighbour. He pointed to a flat-topped mountain very close to the city. 'There's one, see? Pichincha. It's still active.'

'Really?' said Alex, staring at the mountain.

'Oh, yes. They have to close the airport sometimes, when Pichincha's grumbling. The volcanic ash gets in the jet engines and blocks them up. They don't like that.'

Alex smiled and gazed at the volcano, hoping to see a spurt of volcanic ash, but Pichincha sat quietly in the morning sun. The plane dipped lower and lower until Alex could no longer see the mountain tops. It came in low over the fields and paddocks of the fertile lower slopes of the Andes and touched down on the runway of the Aeropuerto Mariscal Sucre as lightly as a feather.

His father was waiting for him in the area just beyond passport control. Alex saw the familiar figure, standing head and shoulders above the crowd, and suddenly, like a thump in the chest, he realized how much he had been missing him. It had been two months since his father had left for Quito with his SAS unit. Their mission was to help the Ecuadorian army to track down and capture a local drugs baron. His father was not in uniform today, though. The unit had been given a week's leave for Christmas, and he was taking Alex to the Galapagos Islands, off the coast of Ecuador.

'Dad!' yelled Alex, beginning to run. 'Over here!'

His father reached out and caught Alex as he skidded to a stop on the marble floor, then grabbed him up in a bear hug. The people around them smiled as they watched father and son, both blond and grey-eyed and both so obviously pleased to see one another.

'OK,' gasped Alex, as his father's embrace threatened to crack a few ribs, 'you can let go now.'

'Still ugly, then?' said his father, standing back and frowning down at him.

'Still old, then?' retorted Alex, scowling back.

His father grinned. 'Come on,' he said, grabbing Alex's bag, 'let's get your horrible face out of here before people start throwing up.'

'Sure you can walk to the car without help?' said Alex.

They left the building and headed for the jeep, trading insults and grinning like a pair of clowns.

'We'll stay in Quito tonight,' Alex's dad explained, once they were on the road. 'Tomorrow, we're driving to Riobamba and catching the train down to Guayaquil. We'll fly from there to the islands. We can ride on the roof of the train, if you want. It's a bit of an adventure.'

'Sounds good to me,' said Alex, settling back in his seat. This was going to be a great holiday.

He looked over to the other side of the road, where a long line of lorries and trucks were queuing to get into the airport. They were all packed full of flowers.

'Some of those flowers'll be on sale in New York before the day's out,' said his father. 'They're a big part of the local economy.'

'Even in December?' asked Alex.

His dad nodded. 'I know it's hard to believe when you can see snow-topped mountains out of the car window, but we're right on the equator here. The thing is, we're also nearly three thousand metres above sea level and that stops the temperatures from getting too high, which means this valley has spring-like weather all year round. And there's a thick layer of rich, volcanic soil on the lower slopes. Perfect for flower-growing.'

'It's like living in paradise,' murmured Alex, gazing at the lorries full of bright flowers.

'Hmm.'

'Hmm?' said Alex. 'What does that mean?'

'It means there's a darker side to this particular paradise. Parts of Ecuador are also perfect for growing coca. Do you know what that is?'

Alex's dad glanced at him and Alex shook his head.

'Well, a coca plant is pretty harmless in its natural state, but if you muck about with it enough, you can turn it into cocaine.'

'Is that what this drugs baron does?' asked Alex.

His father nodded grimly.

'Any luck tracking him down yet?'

Alex's dad sighed and ran a hand through his thick, fair hair. 'He's very difficult to find,' he admitted.

'You'll get him, though,' said Alex.

'Yes,' said his dad, his grey eyes suddenly as hard as steel. 'We will.'

Alex searched for something to say to lighten the mood. He spotted a sad little collection of wilted red roses on the dashboard. 'Looks like you could do with some of those fresh flowers,' he said, picking up one of the brittle stems.

'I buy them from a little girl,' his father said. 'She can't be more than five or six, but she's out on the main road every night, running up to car windows and trying to sell roses.' He shrugged. 'She's a street kid. There are thousands of them here, living rough. Some of them would steal the fillings out of your teeth if they could, but she's – I don't know – different. We'll probably pass her on the road later tonight. I'm taking you into the Old Town. We're having dinner with the guy I'm working with. General Luis Manteca.'

Alex tried to look enthusiastic but he was suddenly overwhelmed by a jaw-cracking yawn. His father laughed. 'It won't be as bad as it sounds. He's a good friend of mine.'

'Sorry,' said Alex. 'We were up most of the night.'

'You and your friends? What were you doing?'

'Oh,' said Alex vaguely. 'Stuff.'

'That's OK,' said his father. 'You don't have to tell me. You're fourteen now. Old enough to have a few secrets.'

Alex grimaced. His dad had no idea what sort of secrets he was keeping these days. Alpha Force had to be kept from their parents, but Alex hated not being able to tell his dad about it. He had always known that there were things about the SAS his father could not discuss with him, but he had never really understood until now how hard it was to keep secrets from the people you loved. Alex could not think of a thing to say, so he covered the silence with another yawn.

'Tell you what. You can have a kip when we get to the hotel,' said his father.

'Hotel?' said Alex. 'I thought we'd be staying at the army base.'

'No way,' said his father with a grin. 'We are starting this holiday in style!'

FIVE

The traffic lights turned to red and the line of cars and taxis heading into the Old Town for the night slowed to a stop. As they waited with their engines idling, a little girl ran out into the middle of the road and held a bunch of red roses up to the driver of the first car. He waved her away.

'Here she comes,' said Alex's dad, pointing through the jeep's windscreen. 'The little girl I told you about. She's here every night. Poor kid.'

Alex watched the girl as she moved from car to car. The headlights showed up the streaks of dirt on her face. One of her sandals flapped loosely from a broken strap and she wore a dirty woollen poncho that was far too big. Her skinny legs stuck out of the bottom of the poncho like matchsticks. Alex had just spent the day in a hotel suite, soaking in a king-sized tub, eating meals brought to him on a tray and sleeping in a clean, warm bed. He felt very lucky and a bit guilty as he watched the girl move along the line of cars towards the jeep.

'Here,' said Alex's father, handing him a dollar bill. 'You can give it to her.'

Alex took the money and wound down the car window. Quick as a mouse, the little girl scurried over to him. Alex picked out a single rose from the bunch she held up and gave her the dollar bill in return.

'*Gracias*,' she said.

'*De nada*,' said Alex's dad, smiling at her. 'You're welcome.'

The little girl stared back solemnly until the lights changed to green, then she darted away towards the pavement.

'She never smiles,' said Alex's dad, shaking his head as he drove away.

A few minutes later the jeep pulled up in front of a neat little Spanish-style house in the Quito suburbs. Alex saw three men standing outside the house, talking. Two of them wore cheap-looking civilian clothes and kept sending uneasy glances up and down the quiet street, as though they felt out of place. The third, a handsome, dark-haired man in his thirties, was dressed in olive-green army fatigues. He looked up at the jeep and touched a hand to the peak of his cap in greeting.

'That's Luis,' said Alex's dad, raising a hand in return.

'But – he's young!' exclaimed Alex.

'Oh, I see,' said Alex's father, pretending to be hurt. 'He's young, but I'm old.'

'I mean, he's young to be a general.'

'Yeah, I thought that too when I first met him. Once I got to know him, it didn't seem so strange. He's very good at what he does. He can stand back and make excellent tactical decisions, but his men would do anything for him because he faces the same dangers as them out in the field. He lives very modestly, too. This is his house – not exactly the house of a general, is it?'

Alex looked out at the little house, then over to Luis Manteca. He had turned back to the men and was counting out dollar bills. The men shoved the money into their pockets and hurried off up the street.

'You must be Alex,' said General Manteca, coming over to the jeep and giving him a firm handshake through the open window. He spoke excellent English with a strong American accent.

'Who were they?' asked Alex's dad, nodding after the men.

'Informers,' said the general. 'My ears on the street.'

'Anything useful?'

'I'll tell you over dinner,' said the general, sprinting round to the other side of the jeep and yanking open the driver's door. 'Move over. I'm taking you both to my favourite eating place.'

'Here we go,' grinned Alex's dad.

'What do you mean?' said Alex. Then his head slammed back against the head-rest as the jeep accelerated away with a screech of tyres.

The general drove like everyone else in Quito, using the brake as little as possible and keeping the heel of his hand ready on the horn. He also had an unnerving habit of taking his hand off the wheel to point out the sights of Quito for Alex. By the time the jeep swerved to a halt in front of a small restaurant with an outside terrace, Alex had the arm-rest next to him in a death grip and had to force himself to let go.

The restaurant was as modest as the general's house, but it was a friendly place and good, local food was its speciality. The general was well known there and they were given a good table at the front of the terrace. Alex sat back with a glass of chilled juice and watched the people of Quito flow past on the street below.

'I wish I was coming with you to the Galapagos Islands,' said the general. 'It's a magical place. The wildlife is spectacular.'

Alex leaned forward eagerly. 'Is it true you can swim with sea lions?'

'I have done it myself,' said the general. 'And with penguins, too.'

'Penguins?' grinned Alex.

'I was as close to them as we are now,' smiled the

56

general. 'On land, there are iguana lizards and giant tortoises.' He leaned towards Alex. 'I could show you a beach, off the tourist route, where hundreds of green sea turtles come to lay their eggs in the moonlight.'

'Wow!' said Alex, caught up in the general's enthusiasm. 'Why don't you come with us? You won't be working over Christmas, will you?'

The general leaned back and shared a look with Alex's dad. 'Unfortunately, I have something else to do. We are tracking a consignment of concentrated sulphuric acid. There are five drums of it on a truck which is driving south through Colombia right now. The truck should cross the border into Ecuador some time later tonight.'

'Sulphuric acid?' asked Alex. 'Why is that so important?'

'It's a vital part of the cocaine production process,' explained Alex's dad. 'This is the best break we've had so far. If we can successfully track this consignment of acid to the cocaine factory, then we will catch our drugs baron.' He looked across at the general. 'Sure you can spare me for a few days, Luis?'

'There's nothing you can do right now. We need to keep everything low key. If the drugs baron hears of a bunch of tough-looking gringos hanging around, he might get a little bit suspicious.'

'Yes, but—'

'Don't worry.' The general pointed to the radio clipped to his belt. 'I have two of my best men following this truck. If there are any problems, they will contact me. We will track the consignment to the factory, then keep the whole thing under surveillance until you get back.'

'OK.'

Alex sighed with relief. For a few seconds, he had thought their Galapagos holiday was under threat.

'What about the street-kid connection?' asked Alex's dad. 'Did your informers have anything?'

The general shrugged. 'Just the usual rumours.'

'What rumours?' asked Alex.

'The word on the street is that the drugs baron is using street kids as mules,' explained Alex's dad. 'A mule is someone who carries drugs to dealers and suppliers in other countries. We've heard he might be using young street kids to carry the cocaine because they're less likely to arouse suspicion.'

Alex thought about the little girl with the big, dark eyes who had been selling roses at the traffic lights. He nodded in understanding. Nobody would suspect a little girl like her of drug-smuggling. 'But how does he get the street kids to carry the cocaine?'

The general shrugged again. 'The rumour is, the street kids think they're going to visit some rich Americans who want to adopt them. They're told they're going to end up on a big estate with a huge house and lots of land.' He shook his head and his brown eyes were suddenly full of sadness. 'It's every street kid's dream. Many of them are orphans. They'd give anything to be part of a family again.'

'So,' said Alex's dad, 'when the adoption men come looking for them, the street kids are fighting to be picked.'

'How do they get the drugs across the border?' asked Alex.

'We're not sure,' his father replied. 'But it's easy to imagine how it might happen. Off they go, carrying a beautifully wrapped "gift" for their new family.'

'Only it's cocaine inside the wrapping,' guessed Alex.

'That's what I think. Of course, the kids don't know what's in the parcels.'

'Yeah, but wouldn't street kids just rip them open?'

Alex's dad shook his head. 'The stakes are too high. They wouldn't risk losing the chance to be part of a wealthy family. Once they've served their purpose, they just disappear.'

'What happens to them?' Alex asked, although he thought he knew the answer.

'We think they are murdered,' sighed the general. 'When they don't come back, it fuels the rumours amongst the street kids here that they're living happily with their new, rich families, so the "adoption" men always have plenty of fresh volunteers.'

'Is it worth trying to follow up the rumours?' asked Alex's dad.

The general shook his head. 'Street kids are usually very suspicious of adults, especially when the adult is wearing a uniform. We wouldn't get anywhere near them. Besides, we can't run around investigating every rumour. The streets are full of them. There's a very persistent one about some guy called the Rat-catcher who goes round in a black car with mirrored windows, hunting for street kids to kill.'

Alex stared at the general in shock. 'Does that really happen?'

'I'm sorry to say it does,' said the general softly. 'A number of people here think street kids are little more than rats to be exterminated. But I don't think all the killings are done by one man. They're random killings, done by different groups. I don't think the Rat-catcher really exists – except as a legend in the minds of the street kids.'

'What if we offered a reward?' asked Alex's dad. 'Would the street kids talk to us then?'

The general laughed. 'You'd have them queuing up round the block,' he said. 'And they'd all have a different story to tell you. No, if you want to spend some money on the street kids, make a donation to Sister Catherine's House. That's what I do.'

'Who's Sister Catherine?' asked Alex.

'She's a nun who runs a home for street kids,' explained the general. 'She's a marvel. Does it all on a shoestring. I admire her. So, I help out when I can, with donations. As for tracking down this drugs baron, I think tracking this consignment of acid is our best chance, not chasing street rumours.' The general looked up and rubbed his hands together as huge plates of lamb stew and rice were brought to the table, along with bowls of sweetcorn and a stack of tortillas. 'But enough of this serious talk! Let's eat. And after that, I'll take you on a grand tour of the Old Town!'

Alex looked at the huge plateful of steaming food in front of him, then at the jeep, which was parked at a crazy angle with its rear-end sticking out into the road. He grinned ruefully at his dad and his dad grinned back.

'What's the joke?' asked General Manteca.

'I'm wondering whether I'm going to make it to the Galapagos Islands,' said Alex.

The general and Alex's dad erupted into laughter and Alex joined in. He did not realize how true his words would prove to be.

SIX

The next morning Alex and his father loaded their luggage into the jeep. They were both travelling light, with one rucksack each. Everything else Alex needed was on his belt. There was a single-bladed knife in a leather sheath, and a pouch which held his passport, a tobacco tin and a small plastic case. The tobacco tin contained the survival kit his father had given him and which he carried with him everywhere. It had proved to be a life-saver earlier that year, when the five members of Alpha Force had been stranded on an Indonesian island. The small plastic case was his

Christmas present to his father. It held a collection of beautifully crafted fishing flies, which it had taken Alex months to make.

They set off on the first leg of their journey, towards the train station. They had only been on the road for a few minutes when the cellphone clipped to the car dashboard began to beep. Alex's dad pressed the button which activated the speaker-phone facility.

'Yes?'

'There's trouble,' said a man's deep voice over the speaker system.

'Mike? What sort of trouble?'

There was a pause. 'We don't have a secure line,' said the voice.

Alex's dad cursed. He had left his radio at the base, thinking he would not be using it over Christmas.

'You need to get over here. Now,' continued the voice.

'Where are you, Mike?'

'On the route we drove the other day, remember?'

'I remember. Any particular rendezvous point?'

'You'll know it when you get there,' said the voice. With a click, the phone went dead.

Alex's dad cursed again, then swung the car round in a screeching turn and began to head north out of Quito. 'Sorry, Alex,' he said. 'We'll have to catch a later train. I need to check this out.'

'What's going on, Dad?' asked Alex.

'That was one of my men from the unit. The route he was talking about is the road between Quito and the Colombian border. My guess is there's been some trouble with that consignment of sulphuric acid.'

They saw the smoke when they were still kilometres away. A thick, greasy smudge of it wavered above the road ahead like a black marker flag. Alex's dad put his foot down when he saw the smoke and the big jeep leaped forward, its spinning tyres sending up a cloud of dust.

A few minutes later they arrived at a small truck stop in a remote spot at the side of the highway. It was nothing more than a square of concrete with a toilet hut – a place where tired lorry-drivers could park-up for a few hours of sleep. A temporary checkpoint had been hastily erected across the turn-off, and two Ecuadorian soldiers were guarding it. As soon as they recognized Alex's father, they saluted and raised the barrier.

Alex's father drove through into the truck stop and parked the jeep in grim silence. The oily black smoke was coming from the burnt-out remains of a small truck. As the smoke drifted over the concrete square towards them, Alex caught a scent which was both acrid and sweet, like the smell of meat left too long on the barbecue.

'There's General Manteca,' said Alex, pointing to a familiar figure in olive green. The general was standing beside two humped shapes lying side by side on the concrete. The shapes were covered over with army blankets and the general's face was strained and grey as he stared down at them.

'And there's Mike,' said Alex's father, as a man built like an all-in wrestler emerged from the other side of the burnt-out truck. He opened his car door and stepped out onto the concrete square. Alex started to follow him.

'No. You stay here, Alex,' ordered his dad. 'You don't want to see this.'

Alex sighed and slumped in his seat as his father

hurried towards the big SAS man. They talked for a few minutes, then they both walked over to join General Manteca. The general crouched and folded back the two blankets. Alex sat up to get a better look. He was guessing that the blankets were covering the remains of the two men from the truck, but they were too far away for him to see anything.

Nobody was looking his way, so Alex eased open the car door and slipped out onto the concrete. His father and the general were deep in conversation. Alex took a deep breath and walked quickly across to the burnt-out truck. As he got closer he could feel a wave of heat still coming from the remains of the truck. The concrete all around the vehicle was blackened and the bushes over on the edge of the square were badly scorched. It must have been an intense blaze.

Alex glanced over at the three men once more, then stepped smartly behind the back of the truck. He eased his way along the far side, listening to the creaks and clicks as the twisted metal slowly cooled. The back of the truck had once been boxed in, but all the panels had burned away, leaving only an open metal framework behind the cab. Alex looked in through the framework and saw that the bed of the truck was empty. There was no sign of the five drums of acid the truck had been carrying.

Alex reached the front of the cab and peered round the corner. His mouth went dry as he realized he had guessed right. He could see two men on the ground, half covered by the army blankets. They were both dressed in civilian clothes and they were both very dead. Alex had been expecting to see burned bodies, but these men had been shot at close range, one in the head and one in the chest. The bullets had done a great deal of damage going in and even more damage on the way out. Alex swallowed hard and just managed to keep his breakfast down.

The general was talking in a flat, hopeless voice, very different to the strong, confident way he had talked about the operation the previous night. 'We found their car a little way down the road,' he said to Alex's father. 'They must have been parked up there, keeping an eye on the truck. They ran over here when they saw the flames – and somebody shot them down.' The general's shoulders slumped.

'Two of my best men,' he said. 'They both have families.'

Alex frowned as he watched his father put an arm around General Manteca's shoulders. He had thought that the men under the blankets were the drivers from the truck. He had been wrong, they were General Manteca's men. So where were the truck-drivers? Alex stepped up to the cab and peered in through the glassless window. At first he did not understand what he was seeing. The seats inside the cab were all burned away, leaving nothing but the metal frames and the springs. Balanced on the springs were two large bundles of shiny black sticks. Alex leaned in for a closer look and the smell of barbecued meat hit him full in the face. His eyes widened and his hand came up to his mouth as he realized that the bundles of sticks were the remains of the truck-drivers.

Alex felt his stomach clench as he stared at the curled-up stick figures. They were both hunched forward in their seats, clinging to the steering wheel. He could not understand it. Why had they stayed in the burning cab? Why had they not jumped out before the flames took them? He looked again at their claw-like hands and this time he saw the twisted wire which had been used to tie their wrists to the steering wheel. Alex lunged away from the truck and vomited into the bushes, then he made his shaky way back to the jeep.

He was still shaking when his father and General Manteca walked over to the jeep together a few minutes later. They seemed to be arguing about something. His father gave him a cursory nod, then frowned and looked at his pale face more closely. 'Are you all right, Alex?'

Alex nodded. He did not tell his father what he had done. He felt vaguely ashamed of himself. He had been warned to stay put, but his curiosity had got the better of him. He had wanted to see what the dead bodies looked like and now he thought he would never be able to forget what he had seen. He shuddered. The person who had done that was truly evil – and his father was trying to track that person down. Suddenly, Alex felt very scared.

'They were my men,' the general insisted, hardly noticing Alex. 'I want to go.'

'Luis, I know how you feel,' said Alex's dad. 'But

think about it. The chances are this guy knows what you look like. And Guayaquil's a coastal city – a jumping-off point for the Galapagos Islands. A bunch of gringo tourists aren't going to be out of place there, are they?'

'What's happening, Dad?' asked Alex.

His dad took a deep breath and looked him in the eye. 'One of Luis's men was still alive when he got here.'

'Barely alive,' muttered the general grimly.

'He died within minutes,' continued Alex's dad. 'But before he died he managed to tell Luis that the men who hijacked the truck and took the drums of acid were from Guayaquil. He recognized their accents and the Guayaquil numberplate on the truck. It's a good lead. There's a strong possibility that this cocaine factory is in Guayaquil. It's Ecuador's biggest port. There's a lot of stuff shipping in and out all the time. It makes sense for the drugs baron to have his base there. So . . .'

'So you're going after them,' said Alex flatly.

'Yes. I'm recalling the unit. We're going deep undercover, as tourists. If we can find the cocaine factory, we can still salvage something out of this mess. I'm sorry, Alex. I know how much you were looking forward to our trip.'

Alex nodded. He was terribly disappointed but, after seeing what had been done to those men, he realized that there were more important things at stake than his Christmas holiday.

'It's OK, Dad. I understand. Really, I do.'

'Good lad. I'll just make some arrangements with Mike, then I'll take you to the airport and see if we can arrange you a flight home.'

'There's nobody there, remember? Mum's in Paris for Christmas, with her mates. I could go and stay in Argentina, though, with Paulo and Li.'

'Sure his family won't mind?'

'No. They'd invited me anyway. I can call them on the way to the airport.'

When they got to the airport, they discovered that there was a flight leaving for Argentina in two hours' time. Alex bought his ticket, then he and his dad stood looking at one another in the departure lounge. It wasn't that Alex had nothing to say to his dad. Rather, he had too many big things to say and didn't know where to start. He had seen what this drugs baron was capable of and he knew that his dad could be going into great danger. A deep-cover operation meant that the unit were on their own, pretending to be civilians, with none of the protection and authority that an SAS uniform might give them. Alex knew his dad might not come back from this one.

'Well,' said his dad finally, glancing at his watch, 'I have to be going.'

'OK,' said Alex, looking at his feet.

His dad reached out and ruffled a big hand through his hair, then he lifted Alex's chin and looked into his eyes. 'Still ugly, I see,' he said.

Alex grinned. 'Older by the minute,' he retorted.

His dad smiled. 'Have a good Christmas, Alex,' he said quietly, then he turned and walked away.

Alex sighed and reached into his belt pouch for his passport. His fingers closed around the little plastic case of fishing flies.

'Dad! Wait!'

His father turned as Alex ran towards him.

'Here,' said Alex, pushing the box into his dad's hands. 'This is for you. For Christmas.'

They shared a quick, fierce hug and then his father was gone, disappearing through the doors of the airport terminal without looking back.

Alex wandered over to the check-in desk and flung his rucksack onto the weighing machine. He wished there was some way he could help his dad, but he was just a kid. What could he do? Then, suddenly, he remembered Amber's last words to him before they split up for the Christmas break.

We'll have to find our own mission, she had said. *Keep your eyes open, Alex*. Of course! There *was* a way to help his dad! Alpha Force could investigate the adoption men rumour. The street kids of Quito might not want to talk to adults, but they would talk to a group of kids their own age.

'Any seating preference?' asked the check-in clerk, in a bored voice.

'I don't want a seat,' said Alex, grabbing his rucksack back just before it disappeared along the conveyor belt.

'Excuse me?' said the clerk.

'I've changed my mind!' yelled Alex, running for the phones.

SEVEN

'Thanks for coming,' said Alex that evening. He was once again sitting on the terrace of the general's favourite restaurant, but this time his companions were Amber, Hex, Li, Paulo and Amber's uncle, John Middleton. 'It's not just to help my dad,' he continued. 'If we can find these bogus adoption men, we'll be helping the street kids too. You didn't mind me calling, did you?'

'Are you kidding?' said Amber, flinging the menu down onto the table. 'I've discovered Hex doesn't do holidays. I mean, New York at Christmas, it's pretty spectacular, right? There's skating in Central Park, all the big stores have these amazing Christmas decorations and there are tons of shows on Broadway. What was the only thing Hex was interested in?'

'You tell me,' grinned Alex.

'The local internet café,' hissed Amber. 'Sheesh! I ask you!'

Hex ran his hands through his straight brown hair so that it stood up in spikes. 'We went there once,' he grated, his green eyes flashing. 'And she spilled coffee all over my keyboard.'

'Alex, I have to thank you for calling us,' said Amber's uncle. 'One more day with these two and I might have committed murder.'

'Li nearly did that,' said Paulo.

'What, murdered someone?' asked Amber.

'Yes,' said Paulo, grinning at Li and nodding his head so hard his dark curls bounced up and down.

Li narrowed her eyes at him. 'Paulo told me all about the heated swimming pool on his family ranch,' she explained. 'He didn't tell me it was going to be swarming with local girls, all competing to become Mrs Paulo. They wouldn't stop talking about his gorgeous sexy eyes and his gorgeous curly hair. So-oo irritating.'

'What did you do, Li?' smiled Alex.

'I just pushed one into the pool, that's all,' said Li demurely, but her dark eyes were sparkling and her high cheekbones flushed a rosy pink as she swallowed down a giggle.

'Poor Rosa,' said Paulo, grinning fondly at Li. 'She was wearing an evening gown. And she couldn't swim.'

'Yeah, well, Paulo jumped in and rescued her,' giggled Li. 'And she decided that he must be in love with her. After that, she wouldn't leave him alone for a second.'

'I, too, am pleased that you called, Alex,' said Paulo, in a heartfelt voice.

'No problem,' said Alex.

'I think it's a perfect first mission for Alpha Force,' said Li. 'It's something only a group of kids could do.'

Amber nodded. 'If someone's murdering street kids, we need to stop them. My mom and dad would've approved,' she said. 'Right, Uncle?'

'Right,' said John Middleton.

The waiter arrived and they all ordered the dish of the day, except Amber, who insisted on ordering the local speciality.

'Is the señorita sure?' asked the waiter, looking at John Middleton.

Amber bristled. 'Hey! I ordered it, didn't I?'

'The señorita would enjoy the dish of the day,' insisted the waiter, still looking at Amber's uncle.

'I said, I'm sure,' hissed Amber, glaring at the waiter, who retreated to the kitchens.

'So,' said Amber smugly. 'What next?'

'Well, I suppose we just hit the streets and find out what we can,' said Alex.

'I have been thinking about that,' said Paulo. 'The street children may talk to us more than they would to an adult, but there will still be a barrier there. Unless they think they are talking to one of their own.'

'Ah. You mean we should pretend to be street kids,' said Hex.

'Not all of us,' said Paulo. 'Just one of us.'

'I could do that,' said Amber. 'I speak Spanish.'

'Not like a local,' said Paulo. 'You don't look like a South American either.'

'But you do,' said Li slowly, giving Paulo a serious stare. 'You think it should be you, don't you?'

'Yes,' said Paulo. 'It is the only way to get the – what do you say? – the inside information.'

One by one the others nodded. 'Sounds like a good idea,' said Alex, speaking for them all. 'But are you sure, Paulo? It could be dangerous.'

'I am sure.'

'We can make it safer,' said John Middleton. 'There are such things as covert radios so that we can keep in touch with you. And I could get a tracker device fitted into your belt buckle. That way, we'll always know where you are.'

'That is good,' said Paulo. 'But where would we get such things?'

'I have a friend in Quito—' began Amber's uncle.

'Don't tell me,' sighed Amber. 'He owes you a favour.'

John Middleton smiled at his niece, then turned back to Paulo. 'After the meal, you and I shall pay him a visit.'

'And the rest of us will hit the streets and try to get a feel for what it's like out there,' said Li. 'Find a safe spot for you.'

'We can all meet up back at the hotel at the end of the—' Alex stopped talking in mid-sentence and his eyes widened as he stared out at the street. Suddenly he pushed his chair back and dived under the table.

'Alex, what the . . .?' said Amber.

'Don't look at me,' hissed Alex.

'Come on,' drawled Hex. 'You don't look that bad. It's only one pimple—'

'See that army jeep coming down the street?' interrupted Alex. 'The guy driving it is General Luis Manteca.'

'What's wrong with him?' asked Li.

'Nothing,' said Alex. 'He's a really nice man – a friend of my dad's – but I can't let him see me here. He thinks I'm in Argentina, staying on Paulo's ranch.'

'So what do we do?' said Hex.

'Just keep talking,' hissed Alex. 'Tell me when he's gone.'

They chatted about the weather and watched the

army jeep drive slowly past them. Alex held his breath under the table.

'Uh-oh,' said Hex, after a moment.

'The general's not coming in here, is he?' yelped Alex.

'No, he's gone,' said Hex in a strangely strangled voice. 'But Amber's meal has arrived.'

Alex emerged from under the table. Amber was staring down at her plate with a look of pure horror on her face and Hex was trying very hard not to laugh. Alex made a quick check up and down the street, then he got back onto his chair and stared at Amber's meal. An animal that looked something like a large rat had been skewered, roasted whole, then laid out on a bed of rice.

Amber stared at the creature for a long time, taking in the neat ears, the little curled paws, the tightly closed eyes and the prominent front teeth.

'What is it?' she squeaked.

'*El cuy,*' said the waiter.

'Mmm. Lovely,' said Amber. 'Thank you.'

As soon as the waiter disappeared, Amber rounded on Paulo. 'What's a *cuy*?' she demanded.

Paulo was red in the face from trying not to laugh. He swallowed hard and looked at Amber. 'It is a guinea pig,' he said.

Hex gave a huge snort of laughter and Amber glared at him. 'Guinea pig!' she shrieked. 'That's the local speciality? What is it with these people?'

'Oh, I don't know, Amber,' giggled Li. 'You've eaten worse.'

They all knew what Li was referring to. Amber was a diabetic. She had to inject herself with insulin twice a day and she also had to make sure she ate regular meals, to keep her blood-sugar levels steady. If she missed a meal, her blood-sugar level could become dangerously low, causing a hypo – a dangerous condition with symptoms of sweating, faintness, irritability and dizziness. When they were stranded on the island, Amber had once been forced to eat raw grubs in order to avoid a hypo.

'You promised you'd never mention the grubs!' flared Amber. She pushed her plate away. 'Anyway, I can't eat this.'

'Then we'll get the waiter to bring you something else,' said John Middleton.

'No!' hissed Amber. 'He'd laugh at me.'

'Here,' said Hex, relenting. 'You can share mine.'

'Thanks,' said Amber, beaming.

As they settled down to their meal, Alex looked around the table at the faces of his friends and realized that, for the first time since that morning, he had stopped feeling scared.

'Street kids up ahead,' murmured Li. 'Looks like trouble.'

'Where?' said Alex, moving closer to her.

'See those two boys?' said Li. 'They're building up for a fight.'

Alex went up on his toes and craned his neck to see over the heads of the crowd. A little way ahead, a thin, dark-haired boy of about thirteen with a sore-looking rash around his mouth was repeatedly shoving another boy in the chest.

'I see them,' said Alex and pointed the boys out to Amber and Hex as they came up to join him. The four of them had been walking around the streets of the Old Town for nearly two hours since they had split up from Paulo and John Middleton. They had been looking for the places where the street kids hung out and had been astounded at the sheer numbers begging on street corners, huddled in doorways or trying to sell roses to the crowds of people walking by.

Alex, Hex, Amber and Li had quickly learned that the street kids gathered in tourist areas, so they had headed for one of the biggest tourist attractions in the Old Town, the Plaza San Francisco. On one side of the plaza the twin white towers of the Monastery of San Francisco, the oldest church in Quito, rose into the night sky. The cobbled plaza below was ringed with stalls. Some were selling tacky religious souvenirs, others were hung with colourful woven bags and belts. Beside these stalls, Indian women, wearing dark felt hats, stood impassively as the crowds surged by.

It was the week before Christmas, a time when traditional, life-sized Nativity scenes were installed in churches and public places all over Quito. The Nativity scene at the Monastery of San Francisco was meant to be one of the most spectacular and a constant procession of people were making their way across the plaza and up the steps to see it. Li, Amber,

Alex and Hex were right in the middle of the crowd when the two street kids started to fight. Suddenly, the thin boy gave the other boy an extra-hard push in the chest and he staggered backwards into the crowd. The two boys started fighting in earnest, fists and feet flying, and the four friends found themselves squashed between two layers of people as the crowd in front of them stepped back and the crowd behind them surged forward for a better view.

'Hey! Watch it!' gasped Amber. She hated being in a crush and she was starting to panic, but the fight was over almost as soon as it had begun. The two boys picked themselves up, nodded to one another as though the fight had never happened, then ran off through the crowd. A third boy pushed past Hex and Amber and ran after the two fighters.

'What was that about?' said Li as the crowd moved on, filling the space where the fight had been.

'It was a diversion,' said Hex grimly, patting at the pocket of his jacket. 'My palmtop's gone.'

Li's eyes narrowed. 'They stole it?'

Hex nodded.

'Well, what are we waiting for?' snapped Li. 'Come on!'

Li darted off through the crowd after the three boys with Alex, Hex and Amber at her heels.

'There they go!' shouted Amber, pointing to the steps that led up to the monastery. The three boys were pushing their way through the crowd towards the main doors. Li put on a spurt and reached the bottom of the steps just as the three street kids were about to disappear into the monastery. The thin boy with the rash around his mouth glanced back. His eyes widened for a second as he saw Li and the others charging up the steps towards him, then he scowled, grabbed the other two boys by the shoulders and pushed them ahead of him into the church.

Li bounded up the steps with her long black hair flying behind her. The other three caught up and they raced into the church together. There, they stumbled to a halt and stood, panting. It was quiet inside the huge church. The only noises were the scuff of feet on the creaking wooden floorboards and the sigh of whispered conversations floating up to the high ceiling. The ornately carved roof was lost in gloom and the bare light bulbs gave only a dim glow to the thick gilding which covered the walls of the church. The three street boys were nowhere in sight.

'They must be here somewhere!' shouted Hex, his fingers frantically keying the air as he yearned for the return of his stolen palmtop.

A disembodied 'Shhh!' came floating towards them. As quietly as they could, the four moved into the main part of the church, looking around them. Over in one corner a life-sized Nativity group dressed in traditional local costume stared back at them. There were benches, statues and dark corners everywhere. If the street kids were lying low in here, they had plenty of hiding-places.

'Split up,' whispered Alex.

The four of them spread out in a line and began making their way to the centre of the church, checking every possible hiding-place. They had nearly reached the other end of the church and Hex was groaning in frustration, when Li suddenly gave a wordless yell.

A second later the three street kids exploded out

of a confessional box and pelted towards a tiny door set in the back wall of the church. Instantly, the four of them changed direction and shot out of the little door only metres behind the street kids.

On they ran, following the street kids through narrow, winding cobbled streets. Li was determined to catch them and she seemed to have boundless energy. Whenever the three boys ahead of her turned a corner, she would increase her speed, always managing to get to the corner just before the boys disappeared around the next one. After a while the street kids were glancing over their shoulders more often, as though they could not quite believe they were still being chased. Alex, Amber and Hex panted along behind, doing their best to keep up.

The streets grew narrower and the crowds thinned out. They were into a quieter, residential area where old houses were divided in flats with wooden balconies leaning out over the street. Alex was beginning to get worried. Suddenly he realized that he had no idea where they were. The street they were running along was completely deserted and their footsteps echoed loudly on the cobbles.

'Li,' he gasped, 'perhaps we'd better give up.'

'We'll catch them at the next corner,' promised Li, sprinting on up the steep incline. 'They're just about finished.'

Alex looked ahead at the three running boys. They were beginning to stumble on the cobbles and one was clutching at his side. 'One more corner,' panted Alex, sprinting after Li.

Li was right. When they rounded the next corner, the boys were waiting for them, lined up across the street, with Hex's palmtop lying on the cobbles in front of them. Alex, Li, Hex and Amber came to a stop and stood there, panting, looking between the three boys and the little computer. Amber shifted uneasily. The boys looked strangely calm as they stood there. The expression in their eyes was flat and dangerous.

Hex stared down at his precious palmtop, lying on the damp cobbles. His fingers keyed the air and he took a step forward. The thin boy with the rash also took a step forward and began to talk in Spanish.

'What's he saying, Amber?' said Hex uneasily, looking longingly at his palmtop.

Amber frowned. The Spanish this boy spoke was very different to the Spanish she had been listening to all term on the language-lab CDs. She listened hard, picking out the few words she recognized. 'I think he's telling you that if you try to pick up that palmtop, you'll regret it,' she said.

Hex scowled. 'Huh. What can they do? It's four against three and none of them looks very strong. I'm going to get it.'

Hex stepped forward again and the three boys tensed but did not move. Slowly he bent down and closed his hand around the little computer. There was a metallic *snick* and suddenly three wickedly sharp flick knives were glinting in the hands of the street kids.

EIGHT

The leader raised his hand, preparing to stab Hex in the back of the neck, but Li was too quick for him. Before Amber could even gather breath to scream, Li was flying over Hex's bent back with one leg stuck stiffly out in front of her. The heel of her shoe slammed solidly into the raised arm of the street kid. He yelled in pain as the knife flew from his hand and skittered across the cobbles.

Amber darted in, picked up the knife and threw it up onto a nearby balcony before the street kid could reach it. Meanwhile Li landed, rolled and came up again in one fluid motion. She gave an explosive yell as she twisted on the spot, bringing her leg round and ramming her foot into the belly of the second boy. He doubled over, dropping his knife and Li kicked it out of reach. Then, quick as a flash, the leader snatched the third boy's knife and lunged for Li.

'Look out, Li!' shouted Alex, but he was too late. The boy had grabbed Li from behind. He was holding her around the throat with one arm. The other hand held the sharp flick knife half a centimetre from her eye. Alex's hand jumped to his own knife, in the leather sheath at his belt, then he thought again. There were too many knives flying about as it was.

For a few shocked seconds everyone was still, then the boy spoke.

Amber swallowed and started to translate in a trembling voice. 'He says don't move or—'

'I can guess,' interrupted Li calmly. 'Just do as he says.'

The boy barked an order and the third street kid walked over to Hex and took the palmtop from his hand, before going to help the second boy, who was still curled up on the cobbles, clutching his stomach. Li waited until she felt the boy behind her shift slightly. The pressure of his arm around her neck loosened a tiny amount. That was all she needed.

She snapped her head back, butting him in the nose. The boy gasped and the arm around her neck went slack. She stepped smartly sideways, at the same time snapping her arm up to knock the knife from his other hand. Before he knew what was happening, she had grabbed him and thrown him over her outstretched leg. He landed on his back and, before he could move, Li grabbed his arm and put him into a wrist lock. Finally she fell to her knees on top of him, with one knee digging into his neck and the other into his lower ribs.

The boy lay beneath Li with all the wind knocked out of him and blood pouring from his nose. Amber, Alex and Hex turned to face the other two street kids. Hurriedly the boy holding the palmtop laid it on the ground, then, with one hand raised in a universal gesture of surrender, he pulled the third boy to his feet and stumbled away.

'Li! Are you all right?' asked Amber as Hex retrieved his palmtop and slipped it back into his jacket.

'I'm fine.'

'How on earth did you do that?' asked Alex.

'Easy-peasy,' grinned Li. 'So. What do we do? Call the police?'

'We can't do that,' said Alex. 'We don't want to draw attention to ourselves. I think we'd better just let him go. He looks like he won't give us any more trouble.'

Li shrugged, released the wrist lock and removed her knees from his chest. The boy staggered to his feet, cursing and spitting. He looked at them all with eyes full of hate and growled a few words of Spanish. They looked to Amber for an explanation.

'He said his name is Leo and he won't forget us. I don't think he meant it kindly.'

The boy glared at them one last time, then staggered off.

'That went well,' said Hex sarcastically. 'So much for making contact with the street kids. It looks as though it's all down to Paulo.'

They wandered tiredly through the streets of the

Old Town and eventually found their way back to their hotel. The hotel was a comfortable, colonial-style building on the edge of the Old Town, overlooking a park. The light above the door glowed a welcome as they stumbled towards it.

'I need food,' said Amber. 'And a bath. A nice, hot—'

She came to a halt as a street boy stepped from the shadows. He was one of the older street kids and he stood as tall as Amber. He lifted his arm towards them and they all tensed, waiting for the knife to appear from his sleeve, but he simply held out his hand, palm upwards. His eyes were dull and watery, his hair hung in greasy tendrils and he smelled very bad. He smiled, exposing a mouthful of yellow, rotting teeth. '*Por favor*,' he whined. '*Por favor . . .*'

Alex sighed. He had seen more than enough of the seedy side of Quito for one night. He pulled a handful of coins from his pocket and dropped them into the boy's hand as he walked towards the front door of the hotel. The boy ducked his head in a grateful bow. 'Thanks, Alex,' he said.

'You're welcome,' said Alex absently, then he

froze with his hand on the door. Slowly he turned round and stared at the street kid. The boy grinned back, giving him a second view of those awful teeth.

'Paulo?' said Alex.

Paulo nodded, smiling proudly.

'That's unbelievable!'

Li rushed forward to hug Paulo, then changed her mind. He smelled too bad. 'I think we fooled them,' said Paulo, speaking into a St Christopher medal strung around his neck. The side door of a white van parked nearby slid open and Amber's uncle stepped out with a huge grin on his face.

A few minutes later they were all in the back of the white van. Inside, there were seats for everyone. One side of the van had shelves fitted to it, which held various pieces of electronic equipment. Paulo was sitting by himself at one end of the van. The others were crowded together at the other end, trying not to breathe too deeply.

'What is that smell?' demanded Li.

'You do not want to know,' smiled Paulo. 'Could you hear me?' he asked, holding up the St Christopher medal and turning to Amber's uncle.

'Every word,' said John Middleton, pointing to the receiver on the shelf. 'But you don't need to hold the medal when you talk. It'll pick up your voice very well from under your shirt there.'

'There's a tracker device too,' said Paulo to the others. He pointed to his belt buckle, then smiled at Amber's uncle. 'Show them how it works.'

John Middleton flipped up the lid of a small black box to reveal a screen about the size of a piece of A4 paper. He extended a telescopic aerial from the back of the box and flicked on the screen. A loud electronic beep filled the van and a grid appeared on the screen, with compass bearings and a distance scale in the top corner. A bright green blip was flashing right in the centre of the grid.

'That's me,' said Paulo proudly.

'You two have been busy,' said Amber, looking around the van. 'How did you get all this together so fast?'

'I told you,' said John Middleton. 'I have a friend in Quito and—'

'He owes you one,' finished Amber.

John Middleton gave Paulo a serious look. 'Are you ready?'

Paulo nodded.

'Hang on,' said Li. 'You're not going out there tonight, are you?'

Paulo shrugged. 'It is not as though I have any bags to pack,' he said.

'Now, remember what we talked about,' said John Middleton.

'I remember,' said Paulo. 'If the adoption men exist – if they appear – I am not to go near them.'

'Not under any circumstances,' insisted John Middleton. 'If they're working for the drugs baron, that means they're killers, whatever the street kids think of them. Understand? Stay back until we can pull you out of there. Then we can follow them in the van.'

'Listen, Paulo,' said Alex urgently. 'There's a kid out there called Leo. If you come across him, be very careful. He's a nasty piece of work – and he carries a knife.'

'I will be careful,' said Paulo, reaching for the door of the van.

'Wait,' said Li. She reached out and hugged him fiercely around the neck, ignoring the ripe smell that was coming off him. 'You take care,' she said.

'He won't be completely on his own, remember,' said Hex. 'We'll be trailing him in the van.'

Reluctantly, Li let go of Paulo's neck. 'But – what are you going to do?' she asked. 'Where are you going to go?'

Paulo pulled a bunch of red roses from under the seat. 'I thought I might sell a few flowers,' he said.

NINE

Paulo frowned down at the roses in his hand. He could not understand it. He had been standing at this intersection for two hours and he had not sold a single flower. It had been impossible to talk to any of the other street kids. They were too busy darting back and forth between the cars. They all seemed to be having a lot more luck than he was. One little girl in particular had managed to sell at least a dozen roses. They seemed a decent enough bunch of kids, though, and Paulo had decided to wait until they packed up for the night, then follow them to where they slept.

Paulo yawned hugely and shifted his feet. He looked down the street, checking that the white van was still parked on the corner, two blocks away. He was cold and tired and his legs ached from standing so long. The constant roar of traffic was giving him a headache and the thick fog of exhaust fumes that hung over the intersection was making his eyes and throat sting, but the little girl in the oversized woollen poncho still seemed as fresh as a daisy. Paulo stared at her, wondering how she did it. She couldn't have been more than six years old.

The girl turned her head and gazed at Paulo with big brown eyes. She reminded him of his youngest sister. He smiled at her fondly, and she scowled horribly at him before darting out into the traffic again as the lights changed to red.

Paulo dropped his roses. Quickly, he gathered them up again, then hurried to the nearest car before the lights changed back to green. He stepped up to the window and gave the driver his best smile. The man flinched and slammed down the door locks before roaring off. Paulo slouched back to the kerb with his shoulders slumped and the little girl marched up to him with one loose sandal flapping.

'Hello,' said Paulo.

The little girl scowled. 'Why did you smile at me?'

'Because you remind me of my little sister,' said Paulo.

The little girl stared up at him and her big brown eyes softened. 'And you remind me of—' She stopped in mid-sentence, then recovered herself and looked him up and down disapprovingly. 'You are too big,' she said.

'Pardon me?' said Paulo.

'You are too big to be selling flowers. The drivers think you are going to steal their cars.'

'Really?'

'Look at the rest of us!' said the little girl.

Paulo looked at all the other flower-sellers. It was true. There was not one child above ten years old. Paulo looked down at his flowers. It had seemed such a good way into the street kids' community. Now he felt very foolish.

'You are new,' said the little girl.

Paulo nodded miserably.

'In from the country?'

'Yes,' said Paulo, hoping that was the right thing to say.

'Thought so,' said the girl. 'There's no work here, you know.'

Paulo shrugged. 'My name is Paulo,' he said.

The little girl sighed, then seemed to come to a decision. 'And my name is Eliza,' she said. 'Come with me.'

'Where are we going?' called Paulo, hurrying after Eliza and checking over his shoulder to see that the white van was following him.

'To get some food,' said Eliza. 'You look like you could do with a hot meal.'

She led him through the streets to a small restaurant that was just closing up for the night. A man with a white chef's apron tied around his big belly waved through the window at Eliza, then came to the door, carrying a bowl full of chicken, rice and vegetables.

'There you go, little one. Bring the bowl back when you're finished.'

'Thank you, Oscar,' said Eliza, solemnly accepting the food. 'This is my friend Paulo.'

Oscar grunted and looked suspiciously at Paulo. 'I suppose you want some for him too?' he said.

A few minutes later they were sitting on the kerb opposite the restaurant with a bowl of leftovers each. The chicken was dry and the vegetables overcooked, but Eliza tucked into the food as though it was the most delicious thing she had ever tasted. As she ate, she lectured Paulo with her mouth full, explaining some of the rules of street life.

'Never try to beg at the big fast-food places,' she said. 'They have armed security guards. Keep away from them. The police too. They don't like us. Oh, and never sleep alone. It's too dangerous.'

Eliza scraped her bowl clean and peered at Paulo's half-finished portion. 'Do you want that?'

Wordlessly, he handed it over. Eliza grabbed the bowl, then froze with the spoon halfway to her mouth as a figure stopped in front of her, blocking out the soft light from the restaurant window.

'Leo!' she cried, gazing up at the thin, dark-haired boy towering over her.

Leo? Paulo looked up sharply. This must be the boy Alex had warned him against. Paulo looked him up and down, trying to see whether he was carrying a knife.

Leo drew his foot back and kicked Eliza on the shin. She doubled over in pain, dropping the bowl of food in the dust.

'Hey!' said Paulo, leaping to his feet. Leo ignored him, but Eliza looked up, her brown eyes brimming with tears of pain, and shook her head in warning. Paulo clenched his fists and fumed silently.

'I've been waiting,' growled Leo, glaring down at Eliza.

'I – I was coming to see you, as soon as I had my food—'

'Where is it?' interrupted Leo.

Eliza jumped up, opened the drawstring purse around her neck and pulled out the few dollars she had managed to earn that night. She handed them to Leo, who sniffed, then peeled off one dollar bill and handed it back to Eliza.

'See you tomorrow,' he said, turning away. 'Don't be late.'

Paulo scowled. Knife or not, he was not going to let this piece of dirt walk off with Eliza's money. She had stood at those traffic lights for hours to earn those few dollars. She deserved to keep them. Paulo grabbed Leo from behind, wrapping his big arms around him and pinning his arms to his sides. Leo twisted and kicked, but he was much thinner and smaller than Paulo. Paulo simply squeezed his arms tighter. He had very strong arms and Leo soon stopped struggling. 'Give me the money,' said Paulo.

Leo wheezed and shook his head. Paulo increased the pressure and Leo's hand shot out from his side, waving the dollar bills frantically.

'Thank you,' said Paulo, reaching down with one big hand and grabbing the money. He let Leo go. Leo turned, quick as a snake, and pulled a knife on him.

Paulo took a step back, pushing Eliza behind him. He was vaguely aware of the big white van driving up the street towards them and he cursed. He did not want his cover to be blown. He wanted to stay and make sure Eliza was safe. Quickly, he took a few more steps, pushing Eliza behind him until they were blocking the road. The white van came to a stop behind them. The headlights came on full and the horn sounded, loud and sudden in the quiet street. Leo hesitated, then slipped the knife behind his back as he shielded his eyes with his other hand.

'The van wants to get past,' said Paulo. 'You need to move on.'

Still Leo didn't move. Then the door of the restaurant opened and Oscar stepped out with his meaty arms folded over his belly.

'Are you going to stab me in front of witnesses?' asked Paulo.

The van horn sounded again. Leo scowled and made the knife disappear into his sleeve. 'Later,' he promised, then he ran off up the street.

Paulo sagged with relief, then pulled Eliza to the side of the road and waved the big van on. John Middleton frowned through the windscreen at him until Paulo gave him a thumbs-up, then he idled away up the street and turned the corner.

Paulo opened Eliza's drawstring purse and pushed the money inside. Then he picked up the two bowls and took them over to Oscar. The big man nodded approvingly. 'You can come to my door anytime,' he said, looking from Paulo to Eliza. 'Anytime.'

* * *

'You shouldn't have done that,' said Eliza, later that night.

Paulo jerked awake. 'What?' he muttered.

'You shouldn't have challenged Leo. He won't forget.'

'Why do you give him all your money?' asked Paulo.

'Protection,' said Eliza briefly. 'At least, that's what he calls it. See, he knows something about me . . .'

Eliza hesitated, then rested her chin on her knees and stared out at the rain, trying to decide whether to say any more. Paulo looked out at the rain too, and waited patiently for her to make up her mind. They were settled for the night in one of Eliza's favourite sleeping places, a covered walkway running along the back of one of Quito's many churches. There were at least twenty other street kids lined up on the concrete walkway, wrapped in an assortment of blankets, plastic sacks and pieces of cardboard. More than half of them had plastic bags and bottles of glue or solvent by their sides.

Paulo supposed sniffing glue helped to dull the cold and hunger. He was heartily glad to see that Eliza did not seem to use it. He suspected that those nightly bowls of dried-up chicken were more precious than Oscar could ever know – they were probably the only thing stopping Eliza from sniffing glue.

'What does Leo know about you?' asked Paulo softly.

Eliza looked along the line, making sure everyone else was asleep. 'I've seen the face of the Rat-catcher,' she whispered.

'The Rat-catcher?' said Paulo. 'What's that?'

'He is a man. He hunts street kids.'

'What for?'

'To kill us.'

'What!'

'He thinks we are like vermin. Like rats. He thinks he is cleaning up the streets of Quito.' Eliza gave a shuddering sigh. 'If the other street kids knew I had seen the face of the Rat-catcher, they wouldn't want to be near me. I wouldn't be able to sleep here or work at the traffic lights. They'd make me go away on my own.' Eliza's lower lip trembled as she looked down at her hands.

'Why?' asked Paulo.

'Because they think if you've seen the Rat-catcher, you're as good as dead, and they wouldn't want to be around someone like that. Leo says he'll tell the others if I don't pay him protection money.'

Paulo put an arm around her thin shoulders and she snuggled in against his chest. 'How does Leo know?' he asked.

Eliza looked up at Paulo and he smiled down at her. He looked so much like her big brother Marco when he smiled that she decided to tell him everything.

In the white van, parked at the front of the church, John Middleton was asleep at the wheel, with his mouth open and his head lolling over the back of the seat. Alex, Li and Hex were all sprawled on the seats in the back of the van. Hex was clutching his palmtop close to his chest as he slept.

Amber was the only one awake. She was sitting in front of the radio receiver, listening to Eliza's soft voice as it was picked up by the covert radio in Paulo's

St Christopher medal. Amber's face was a picture of concentration as she translated the Spanish into English. It had been hard work to start with but now she found it was getting easier by the minute. Even so, she was always a few seconds behind.

Suddenly, Amber sat up straight and pushed the headphones closer to her ear, as though that might help her understand more clearly. Her mouth dropped open and her eyes widened in horror as she listened to Eliza's story. 'That poor, poor kid,' she said. 'She saw the Rat-catcher kill her big brother, Marco. It was all that Leo's fault – can you believe that . . .? He led this Rat-catcher guy right to them, then ran away.'

Amber turned to look at the others, but they were all still fast asleep. She waved a dismissive hand at them and turned back to listen to the rest of Eliza's story. As she heard what happened next, her eyes filled with tears. The tears overflowed and dripped down onto the receiver, but Amber did not notice. She was too wrapped up in the story.

Eliza felt her voice begin to wobble as she finished describing how Marco died. She stopped for a moment and Paulo gave her shoulder a reassuring squeeze.

'Leo came back later that night,' she continued. 'He had come to steal my brother's shoe-shine box. He found me and Toby there and he realized we had seen everything. That's when he said I had to pay him for protection. I begged him to leave the shoe-shine box, but he took it away. He had a buyer for it.' Eliza sighed. 'If I'd had the shoe-shine box, I could've earned enough to rent a room. I could've kept Toby with me. Instead, I had to leave him on the doorstep at Sister Catherine's House. He cried so much, but I had to leave him.'

'But why didn't you stay there too, Eliza?'

'No. Toby will be better off without me.' Eliza scrubbed the tears from her face and tried to smile. 'I think Toby will be adopted by now. He will be with a good family! He is light-skinned, you see, with curly blond hair. Not like me.'

'Eliza, you're beautiful—'

'No. I am *morena*. I am dark-skinned. The rich people who go to Sister Catherine's House looking for children to adopt, they do not want *Indio* children.'

'Not everyone is so prejudiced, Eliza,' said Paulo.

'I know that now,' said Eliza, a flicker of hope coming into her eyes. 'The adoption men who come looking for street children, they do not mind what colour our skin is!'

'Adoption men?' asked Paulo, careful to keep the excitement out of his voice.

'Yes. They come every two or three weeks. Everybody wants a chance to go with the adoption men, but each time they take only two lucky ones away with them. The adoption men have rich people queuing up to adopt street kids, even *mestizos* like me. The kids who go with the adoption men, they end up in a big house on a big estate.'

Eliza turned her shining face up to Paulo and the hope in her eyes nearly broke his heart. 'One day,' she said, 'the adoption men will take me. Then my new family will help me to find Toby and we will be together again.'

Eliza closed her eyes and snuggled against Paulo's chest as she imagined that wonderful day. Paulo nearly told her the truth about the adoption men, but he decided it could wait until the next morning.

Instead, he held Eliza close and let her drift off to sleep with her dreams still intact. He had no idea how much he would later regret that decision.

TEN

Paulo woke with a start as someone kicked the sole of his boot. His eyes snapped open but he shut them again almost immediately. A blinding light was shining straight into his face. 'Who's there?' he demanded.

Eliza woke and sat up, instantly alert, like a cat.

'I said I'd see you later,' said a soft, sinister voice behind the light. 'Well, it's later now.'

'Leo,' whispered Eliza.

'And a few friends,' said Leo.

Paulo did not wait to be attacked. He lunged to

his feet and ran full tilt straight into Leo. The torch went flying onto the concrete floor and shattered, plunging the back of the church into darkness. Leo crashed to the ground and Paulo scrambled to his feet, desperately trying to see something beyond the bright red ring burned into his retinas by the torch.

'Get him!' yelled Leo, from the ground.

Paulo thought he could see four dark shapes coming towards him. He stuck his arm out to the side, feeling for Eliza, and she slipped her small hand into his. Paulo took a deep breath and ran, dragging Eliza along behind him. He felt hands grabbing at his clothes but he kept on going, running blind. He had nearly reached the corner when Eliza's hand was suddenly snatched away.

'Paulo!' she screamed.

Paulo groaned and turned back to face their attackers. His vision was beginning to clear now. He could see one boy holding a struggling Eliza against the wall of church. He took a step towards her but three more boys jumped him from behind. One grabbed his hair, a second bent his arm up behind his back until he thought the bone would crack and the third pressed the point of a knife into the small of his back. Paulo froze in place.

A few metres away Leo was clambering to his feet. He straightened and looked at Paulo with hatred. *Snick*. The sharp blade of the flick knife appeared as Leo walked towards Paulo. 'Time for some carving,' he snarled.

Finally Paulo remembered the covert radio around his neck. He knew it was his only chance. He filled his lungs and yelled for help at the top of his voice.

In the van Amber had dozed off in her seat with the headphones still clamped to her head. She jolted awake, with Paulo's shout ringing in her ears. '*Socorro!*' That meant 'help'.

Amber ripped the headphones off and dived towards the front of the van. Frantically she grabbed the sleeping John Middleton by the shoulder and shook him hard. 'Paulo's in trouble!' she screamed.

The other three in the back of the van woke up as Amber grabbed the headphones again. A look of horror crossed her face as she listened. 'It's Leo,' she whispered. 'Leo's got him.'

John Middleton grabbed the ignition key and started the engine. The van had been left in gear, so it instantly lurched forward and stalled. With a curse, he tried again. The engine coughed but would not start.

'*Socorro!*' yelled Paulo again, his voice filtering faintly into the van through the headphones.

'We'll run,' said Li, jumping for the side door of the van.

'Hang on!' called John Middleton as the engine finally started. The van shot forward, accelerating all the time. It took the first corner on two wheels, righted itself and careered along the street that ran down the side of the church. They were heading for the road that led to the back of the church, but John Middleton slowed the van as he spotted a pair of red tail-lights between the buildings. Another car had already beaten them to it.

'What the hell is going on?' demanded Li.

Amber clamped the earphones to her head, listening intently. 'I can hear Eliza,' she said. 'She's shouting something about being saved. Something about— Oh no! She says it's the adoption men.'

* * *

Paulo let out a sigh of relief as the headlights finally appeared behind him. Leo had been getting ready to slice the knife into his cheek. The boy holding Eliza let her go and ran off. One by one the three boys holding Paulo lost their nerve and followed the first boy, but Leo was not giving up that easily. As Paulo backed slowly towards the headlights, Leo followed him, step by step, throwing his knife from hand to hand.

Eliza peered into the headlights, then her face lit up. 'Paulo! We are saved!'

'Not yet,' muttered Paulo, watching Leo's knife.

'It's the adoption men!' cried Eliza.

'What?' Paulo twisted round and stared into the headlights. An old Chevrolet was parked at the end of the street, not the white van he was expecting. Two men clambered from the car and Eliza ran towards them.

'Take me,' she cried. 'Me and my brother Paulo. Please?'

One of the men shrugged. They had been about to check out the covered walkway and take their pick of the street kids sleeping there, but these two were as good as any other pair. Besides, the boss liked brothers and sisters. The bond made them easier to control. He nodded towards the car and Eliza ran for the open back door.

'Wait, Eliza!' called Paulo, but Eliza was already climbing into the back of the car.

The man looked past Paulo to Leo, grimacing as he saw the glue-sniffer's rash around the boy's mouth. Quickly, Leo slipped the knife into his sleeve and arranged his face into a strange sneer. Paulo realized with a jolt of angry pity that Leo was trying to look appealing.

'Maybe next time,' the man said to Leo dismissively. 'Off you go, son.'

Leo glowered at Paulo, then limped away as the man turned to Paulo. 'Get in, then,' he said.

The man turned away, heading for the car. Paulo hesitated, trying to decide what to do. He was under strict instructions not to go with the adoption men, but he couldn't let Eliza go off with them on her own. Perhaps the best thing would be to go along with it, pretending he was as pleased as Eliza to be picked. After all, the men would not try to kill them before they had delivered the cocaine, so that gave him time to work out a way to escape.

'Come on, son!' called the man. 'We haven't got all night.'

Paulo nodded and started walking slowly towards the car. On the way, he hooked out his St Christopher medal and raised it to his lips. He whispered a few words into it and kissed the medal as though he had been saying nothing more than a quick prayer for a safe journey. Letting the medal drop back into his shirt, Paulo climbed into the back of the car.

John Middleton had brought the van to a halt by the side of the road.

'Don't stop!' cried Li frantically. 'We have to get to Paulo!'

Alex shook his head. 'It's not that simple. He's not in danger from Leo now, and if we barge in there, we might be putting everyone's lives at risk. Those men might have guns. We have to trust Paulo to tell us what to do.'

For a few agonized seconds they waited, staring at

Amber. She pressed the headphones to her ear, willing Paulo to say something. Finally she heard his whispered words and turned to look at the others. 'Paulo says we have to stay back and follow the car.'

'The idiot!' fumed Li. 'Why is he going with them?'

'He said he has to protect Eliza,' said Amber.

'The idiot!' repeated Li fiercely, but her chin was trembling as she said it.

The old Chevrolet reversed out of the side road and headed off into the night. John Middleton sat at the wheel, watching as the car turned a corner further down the road. Only then did he start the van's engine and turn on the headlights.

'Come on then!' yelled Li. 'We're losing them!'

'No we're not,' said Hex, activating the tracking device. 'We've got this.'

The streets of the city were early-morning quiet so they kept well back. Hex watched the green blip on the screen and called directions to John Middleton. It was unnerving, following a car that they could not actually see, but the signal was clear and the bleep was strong.

Suddenly, Hex frowned down at the screen. 'Slow down,' he ordered.

'What is it, Hex?' asked Amber.

'They've stopped,' said Hex. 'The car's stopped.'

John Middleton killed the headlights and carefully eased the van to the edge of the junction. Quietly he brought the van to a halt and turned off the engine. The Chevrolet had stopped further along the road, outside a small, newly built block of flats.

'He looks OK,' whispered Alex as they watched Paulo clamber out of the car, then reach in to help Eliza. They saw him glance along the street, checking that the white van was there. The two adoption men climbed out of the car and, as they turned their faces his way, Alex frowned. Those two men looked vaguely familiar to him but he could not think why.

Paulo and Eliza followed the men to one of the ground-floor flats. One of the men unlocked the door and they all went in.

'What's happening?' asked Li, looking at Amber.

'Eliza's happy,' said Amber, listening to the

headphones. 'She's bouncing on the bed, I think . . . There are new clothes for her . . . and, oh, she's found the bathroom. She's turning on the taps. She keeps saying, "Hot water . . . hot water . . ." as though she can't quite believe it. Hang on, Paulo's shooing her out of the bathroom. He's locking the door.'

Amber stopped and listened intently to Paulo's whispered instructions. Finally she pulled the headphones down around her neck. 'Paulo says everything is fine. He says they're in no danger as long as he pretends he's happy to be there. The men have told him that their boss will arrive in the morning, to take him and Eliza to the airport and put them on a plane to visit their new parents. Paulo is planning to go with the drugs baron to the airport, then report him to the airport police and get him arrested.'

Hex nodded. 'Good plan,' he said. 'He's not nearly as dumb as he looks.'

'So, what do we do?' asked Li, giving Hex a poisonous stare.

'We wait,' Alex replied.

'I agree,' said John Middleton. 'But not here. This

is a busy junction. Once the morning traffic gets going we won't be able to stay here.'

'But we can't park outside the flats,' said Amber. 'They might get suspicious of a van pulling up at this time of night.'

'We could park in the next road down,' said Hex. 'It's only a couple of minutes away – and we've got the radio receiver and the tracking device to keep tabs on Paulo.' He looked enquiringly at the others and one by one they nodded their agreement. John Middleton started the engine and the white van drove off to park in the next road. It seemed like a sensible plan, but Alpha Force had just made a very big mistake.

ELEVEN

Paulo was as tense as stretched wire. They had spent the remains of the night at the flat and now the morning was ticking by and still the boss had not arrived. Eliza was happy. She was wearing a new dress, her hair was freshly washed and her belly was full of breakfast. She was standing at the bedroom window, waiting impatiently for the boss to turn up and take them to the airport.

Paulo sat down on the bed and stared at the bag of festively wrapped 'presents' he and Eliza were supposed to hand over to their prospective new parents. If each of those presents held blocks of cocaine, then he was looking at a bag that was worth millions of dollars. When they handed over the bag of presents, their 'parents' would give them a wrapped Christmas parcel in exchange, which Paulo was under strict instructions to bring back unopened. He guessed that the parcel would be full of high-denomination bills.

Paulo shook his head as he eased the scratchy collar of the cheap new shirt away from his neck. He had to admit, it was a brilliant drug-smuggling technique. The airport staff and the flight assistants on the plane would never suspect two happy kids with an armful of presents. The fact that the kids did not know what they were carrying onto the plane only made the deception more convincing. And the street kids would be on their best behaviour because they wanted their prospective new parents to like them. Once they arrived back in Quito with the money, they were killed. It was as simple as that. There would be no evidence, no tell-tale trail leading back to the drugs baron. Street kids were disappearing all the time. Nobody would miss a few more.

As Paulo stared at the brightly wrapped presents, he realized that it was the weekend before Christmas. Back home in Argentina, his family would be preparing the ranch for the big party they always held. Paulo had a sudden fierce desire to be with his family instead of stuck in a poky bedroom in Quito, waiting to meet the most dangerous drugs baron in Ecuador.

Suddenly, Eliza started jumping up and down at the window. A car had just pulled up outside the flat. 'He's here! He's here!' she squeaked, turning to Paulo in excitement as the man climbed out of the car.

Paulo stood up and straightened his shoulders. It was show-time. He looked out of the window and felt a jolt of shock run through him as he saw the face of the man walking up the path. Paulo recognized him. He had watched this man drive a military jeep past the restaurant terrace where Alpha Force had been sitting only the day before. The man was in civilian clothes now, but there was no doubt in Paulo's mind.

He was looking at General Luis Manteca.

Eliza saw the expression on Paulo's face and turned back to the window to see what had shocked him so much. She gave a frightened whimper as she too saw the face of the man walking up the path. Her eyes grew wide and she began to shake all over. She did not know this man as General Manteca. She only had one name for him. The Rat-catcher. He was the Rat-catcher who had murdered her brother. Eliza began to scream.

'Can't we get some fresh air in here?' grumbled Amber, as a drop of sweat fell from the end of her nose. The inside of the white van was becoming hotter by the minute as the sun rose higher in the sky

'Good idea, Amber,' said Hex. 'Why don't we just fling the side door open and let everyone see us all sitting in here with our surveillance equipment?'

'Shut up, would you?' sighed Amber, pulling the headphones from her ears and slamming them down onto the radio receiver.

'Keep them on, Amber!' snapped Li.

'You keep them on!' retorted Amber.

'Amber, you're the only one who understands Spanish,' said Alex tiredly.

'All right! All right, Mr Logical!'

Amber slouched back in her seat and lifted her

hair away from her sweaty neck. 'Just give me a minute,' she muttered. 'I need a break from listening to Little Orphan Annie prattling on about how wonderful her new parents are going to be.'

Li stood up and pushed her head up into the open skylight window, trying to find some cooler air. She cocked her head and listened. 'Can you hear that?' she asked.

'It's him,' said Amber, pointing at her uncle, who was sprawled out on the front seat of the van, snoring gently.

'No, not the snoring,' said Li. 'Listen.'

They all concentrated.

'It's music,' said Li.

'Somebody's playing Christmas carols,' said Alex.

'Very badly,' added Hex.

'Where's it coming from?' asked Li.

Amber tipped her seat back and craned her neck to look out of the front windscreen of the van. She nearly fell out of her chair when a high scream exploded from the headphones on top of the receiver. Lunging forward, she grabbed the headphones and slammed them back onto her head. She listened for a few seconds and her eyes grew wide with shock.

'The drugs baron has arrived at the flat. Eliza is screaming. She says the drugs baron is the Rat-catcher – and Paulo says it's . . . he says it's General Manteca! They're in trouble!' she yelled. 'We have to get over there. Now!'

Eliza's screams filled the tiny bedroom of the flat. Paulo grabbed her and tried to cover her mouth but she tore his hand away. 'It's the Rat-catcher!' she screamed hysterically. 'The Rat-catcher!'

Paulo ran to the bedroom door and yanked it open just as the general burst into the flat. The two adoption men ran from the kitchen, their faces slack with shock. For an instant, everyone was still. Then Eliza screamed again from the bedroom behind Paulo.

'It's him. The Rat-catcher!' she sobbed. 'He killed my brother! I saw him!'

Paulo froze in the doorway as the general turned to look at him with the coldest pair of eyes he had ever seen.

'Shut them up,' the general ordered his men. 'Now!'

The two men sprang down the corridor towards Paulo. He jumped back into the bedroom and slammed the door shut. He looked frantically around the little room, then grabbed a nearby chair and wedged it under the door handle.

'The drugs baron is here!' he shouted into the medal around his neck as he ran for the window. 'It's the general! Do you understand? The drugs baron is General Luis Manteca!'

Paulo reached the window as the door handle started rattling. He yanked the blind away from the frame and grabbed the lever to open the window. It was locked. Behind him, the door handle stopped rattling. A second later there was a huge thud as someone threw themselves against the other side of the door. Eliza screamed again and squeezed herself into the furthest corner of the room like a frightened animal.

'We need help, now!' yelled Paulo as he picked up a flimsy bedside table and started pounding it against the window. 'The general. The drugs baron. The Rat-catcher. They're all the same man! Do you hear me? They're all the same man – and he's breaking down the door right now!'

The little table splintered into pieces in Paulo's hands. The window was not even cracked. Paulo threw the remains of the table to the floor, then changed his mind and picked up the splintered leg. He turned, holding the frail stick of wood in his fist, as the bedroom door was smashed open.

The general walked calmly into the room, with his two men behind him. Paulo looked into his smiling, cruel face and felt a cold chill run down his back. There was no mercy in the general's eyes, only a deep, disturbing madness.

As the white van lurched away from the kerb and screeched down the road, Amber disconnected the headphones and flicked a switch on the radio receiver so that everyone could hear what was happening to Paulo and Eliza.

'The general is the Rat-catcher?' gasped Alex, grabbing onto a shelf as the van slewed round a bend. 'And the drugs baron, too? Are you sure you've got that right, Amber?'

Amber nodded. 'Pretty sure. He's a busy man.'

Alex shook his head in disbelief. 'It can't be the general. Hang on, though, maybe he's come to rescue them!'

Alex looked at the others with a hopeful expression. Just then they all heard the general shout an order over Eliza's high screams.

'He's telling his men to hold the boy,' said Amber. 'He's—' Amber stopped. There was no need to explain what was happening. They could all hear Paulo's grunts of pain echoing from the receiver. Li flinched as a sharp slap made Paulo cry out. She looked out of the front windscreen of the van. They were heading for the junction which would take them the short distance to the flats. The traffic lights were on red but there was no sign of any traffic crossing the junction ahead.

'Jump the lights,' ordered Li. 'We have to get to Paulo.'

John Middleton nodded, and put his foot down on the accelerator. The van slewed out of the junction, then screeched to a halt in the middle of the empty road.

'This can't be happening,' whispered Li, as she stared at the road ahead. No wonder there had been no traffic crossing the junction. A marching band was heading down the road towards them, followed by a huge crowd of people, all dressed in traditional costume. The band was playing Christmas carols and, at the head of the crowd, a line of men were carrying a group of life-sized Nativity figures on their shoulders. Behind them, the crowd stretched back along the road as far as Li could see.

Suddenly a crunching sound came from the receiver, followed by a whine of feedback. Then the radio fell silent. Amber grabbed the receiver and began to twist the dials, trying to find Paulo again, but it was useless.

'We've lost contact,' said Amber.

'That's it!' hissed Li. 'I'm not sitting here a second longer!'

The four of them left John Middleton in the van and ran as fast as they could towards the flats. Within seconds they were in the thick of the happy crowd and fighting their way through the dancing, twirling figures. Amber collided with a small, wheeled sweets stall, picked herself up and stumbled on, trailing streamers of pink candyfloss from her hair. As they ran and dodged, Alex could not stop the same shocked thought running through his head. General Manteca! It was General Manteca all along!

After endless minutes of barging and pushing, they broke out of the tail-end of the parade. The street junction leading to the flats was only metres ahead of them. Li put on a spurt even though her lungs were burning. She turned the corner and pelted towards the flats but her heart was sinking inside her. She could see that the front door of the flat was swinging open and there was no sign of the old Chevrolet.

'Wait!' panted Alex, grabbing Li by the shoulder as she was about to burst through the open front door into the flat. Li struggled briefly, then came to her senses. They waited for Hex and Amber to catch up, then edged into the dim passageway. Alex saw three doors leading from the passageway, all open. He gestured silently, indicating that Amber should stay at the front door.

The first door opened into a kitchen. Alex could

see a fridge and the corner of a kitchen table. He gestured to Hex, who nodded and padded silently up to the door. He eased his head round, then turned to Alex with an all-clear signal. They moved on down the corridor. The bathroom was empty too. That left only one door. Alex took a deep breath and slipped through the open doorway. It was a small bedroom and it was empty.

Alex stepped further into the room and a cold chill settled in his stomach as he saw the destruction there. The remains of a small table littered the floor, a chair lay on its side and the blinds had been ripped from the window. There were smears of blood over the cover of the nearest bed and blood was also spattered across the floor. As Alex stared at the blood, he caught sight of something shiny under the bed. He leaned closer and picked it up. Wordlessly he held it up for the others to see. Swinging from a broken chain were the smashed remains of Paulo's covert radio.

'Oh, no,' moaned Li.

A blaring horn shattered the quiet. They ran out into the street. The white van was outside, with its engine revving.

'Come on!' called John Middleton through the van window. 'I've got a signal!'

They tracked the signal through the city for nearly twenty minutes, jumping red lights all the way. 'It's the airport,' said Alex finally, spotting a sign up ahead. 'We're heading towards the airport. That's where they're taking him!'

'They're not taking him,' said Hex, staring at the green blip on the tracker screen. 'They've already arrived. The signal has stopped moving.'

The van speeded on, following Hex's directions, and the beep from the tracker grew louder and stronger by the second. Finally the airport complex came into view.

'OK,' said Alex. 'When we get to the terminal, we split up and quarter the building. We'll keep in touch via our cellphones.'

'And I'll stay here and monitor the tracker,' said John Middleton, slewing the van round the corner to the front of the terminal building.

'I think we're too late,' said Hex quietly.

'What do you mean?' demanded Li.

Hex turned the screen so that they could all see it.

The green blip showed that Paulo was on the move again.

'He's already on a plane,' said Hex.

'What!' shrieked Li. 'How do you know?'

Hex nodded at the blip on the screen. 'No car could go at that speed.'

'But – there are planes taking off all the time! How do we know which one Paulo's on? How do we know?'

'We don't,' said Alex flatly.

The tracker only had a five-kilometre range. They sat in the van and watched in horror as the little green blip faded and disappeared.

'This wasn't supposed to happen!' yelled Amber. 'What are we going to do? We have to find him!'

'Satellite tracking,' said Hex suddenly. He turned to John Middleton. 'A satellite could track that signal for us, couldn't it?'

John Middleton nodded, his face lighting up with a wary hope. He wrestled his cellphone from his pocket and began to dial a number.

'What are you doing?' asked Hex.

'I have a friend who works for NASA—' he replied.

'And he owes you a favour,' finished Amber.

Ten minutes later the white van was heading back into Quito centre. John Middleton had made arrangements for his friend to fax the satellite pictures to him at the hotel as soon as they were ready, but it was going to take a couple of hours.

'Two hours,' groaned Li in the back of the van. 'The general could do anything to them in that time. What if he . . .?' Li swallowed, then tried again. 'What if he kills them?'

'Don't think about that,' said Alex firmly. 'The general doesn't know he's got us on his tail. We'll get to Paulo and Eliza in time.'

'But what about the radio?' said Amber. 'What if it wasn't smashed by accident?'

Hex shook his head. 'If the general had found the radio, he would have found the tracker device too. But the tracker device is still working. I think Alex is right. The general doesn't know about us.'

Li looked at each of the others in turn, then she bit her lip and gazed down at the floor, trying not to cry. Amber reached out and rested her hand on Li's arm. They lapsed into silence, each struggling with their own thoughts about what the general might be doing to funny, gentle Paulo. Alex clenched his fists in frustration. There was nothing Alpha Force could do until the satellite images came in. He stared out through the windscreen of the van and his eyes widened as he suddenly recognized where they were. Perhaps there was something Alpha Force could do, after all.

'Can you let us out here?' he said, with elaborate casualness. 'I need to stretch my legs a bit after being cooped up in this van all night.'

'Good idea,' said John Middleton as he brought the big van to the side of the road. 'I'll call Amber when the satellite pictures are in.'

'So. What are we really going to do?' asked Amber as they watched the white van speed off down the road.

'A bit of breaking and entering,' said Alex.

TWELVE

The street was deserted when Alex peered around the corner. He was counting on it staying that way. It was the last Saturday before Christmas. Most people would be out shopping.

'Which house is it?' whispered Amber, peering over his shoulder.

'Third one along on the left,' said Alex. 'The one with the garage on the side of the house.'

'Are you sure it's the general's house?' asked Hex.

'I'm sure. My dad and I picked him up from here just two nights ago. He was actually talking to those two adoption men when we arrived – paying them off, as cool as you like, and telling my dad they were his "ears on the street".' Alex let out an exasperated sigh as he remembered. 'I knew they looked familiar! That guy is so sure of himself.'

'Too sure, if you ask me,' said Hex. 'Someone's going to catch him out one of these days.'

'How are we going to reach the house?' asked Li.

'We walk up to it, of course,' said Alex.

'What? In full view?'

'We're just kids, remember,' said Amber. 'Who's going to take any notice of a bunch of kids?'

'Blinds are down,' muttered Li as they headed up the road towards the house. 'How do we know he hasn't come back here?'

'We don't know for sure,' said Alex. 'But we have to try to get in. We might find something in there that leads us to Paulo.'

'The house is alarmed,' said Hex, assessing the security. 'But I'll bet the garage isn't – and there might be a connecting door. I think we should go in through the garage. Those trees and bushes are going to give us a fair amount of cover.'

When they reached the top of the driveway, Hex took one look at the garage doors and sneered. 'See what I mean?' he whispered. 'Too sure of himself.'

They were a pair of old-fashioned wooden doors and the only thing holding them shut was a wrought-iron drop-latch. Hex gripped the latch and eased it up, then he gently tugged one of the doors. The rusting metal hinges squealed loudly and a whole flock of small birds exploded from the garden trees. Amber grabbed Alex's arm, digging her fingernails into his skin.

Hex took a quick look down the driveway to the street, then he slipped into the dark garage. Li followed, then Alex, with Amber crowding in behind him.

'There's a car in here,' said Hex.

Amber gave a squeak of panic. 'He must be in the house!'

'No, I don't think so,' said Li, running her finger over the tarpaulin that covered the car. 'Look. Dust. This has been here for quite a while.'

Alex lifted a corner of the tarpaulin and pulled it back. A shiny black bonnet came into view, then a dark windscreen. Amber peered at the windscreen and gasped in shock as she saw a face staring back at her.

Someone was sitting in the car.

She took a step back, preparing to run, but Alex reached out and squeezed her wrist reassuringly. 'It's all right,' he said calmly. 'It's mirrored glass.'

Alex pulled the tarpaulin further back, flicking it up and over the halogen lamps on the top of the 4x4. He nodded grimly. Eliza was right. The general was the Rat-catcher, and they had just found his hunting machine.

'Over here!' called Li softly.

The other three edged round the big car to join her. She was standing in front of a door in the side wall.

'Told you,' said Hex smugly.

The door had a pull-down handle, with a simple, keyhole lock. Hex peered into the keyhole and grunted in satisfaction. 'Key's in there,' he said. 'On the other side.'

He hurried over to a workbench against the wall and grabbed an old newspaper and a length of thick wire. He opened up a sheet of the newspaper and slid it under the door, leaving a small edge remaining on the garage side, then he eased the wire into the keyhole and slowly pushed the key out of the lock. The key dropped onto the newspaper sheet on the other side of the door.

'Now for the tricky bit,' said Hex. 'I just hope the gap's big enough.' Slowly he pulled the news-paper sheet back through into the garage. The key came with it, sliding under the bottom edge of the door with less than a millimetre to spare.

'Yes!' smiled Hex, snatching up the key. He slipped it into the keyhole, unlocked the door and pulled down the handle. The door opened silently outwards, into the garage. The blinds were down in the room beyond the door, but there was enough light to see that it was a kitchen. There was a cooker, a fridge and fitted cupboards with wooden, latticework doors. Hex looked over at the bench opposite the door and his eyes lit up as he spotted an expensive laptop plugged into the phone socket.

'Bingo,' he said.

Li sprang for the step but Hex grabbed her round the waist and pulled her back. 'What now?' hissed Li impatiently.

'The house is alarmed, remember?' said Hex.

'All right, Hex,' said Alex. 'You're our security expert. What do we do?'

Hex scanned the garage until he spotted what he wanted. Grabbing a large chisel from the workbench, he walked over to the exposed side of the 4x4. He rammed the chisel in behind the wing mirror and levered it until the whole thing came away from the side of the big car. Hex turned back to the other three with the wing mirror in his hand and raised an eyebrow at their shocked faces. 'Hey. This is war, remember,' he reminded them.

He angled the wing mirror in the kitchen doorway until he could see the hidden, near corner of the room. 'There it is,' he muttered. 'Motion-detector, above the bench.'

'Is there a way to beat it?' asked Alex.

'In theory, yes.' Hex went back to the workbench, picked up an aerosol can of car polish and shook it. 'We use this.'

'Oh, right,' mocked Amber. 'Give it a good polish. That'll do it every time.'

'It's a foam polish,' said Hex. 'If you spray any

sort of foam over a motion-detector it blocks the beam and puts it out of action.'

'But how do we get near enough to spray it?'

'That's the dodgy bit,' admitted Hex. 'The trick is to move really, really smoothly and slowly. Less than a couple of centimetres a minute. If you move slowly enough, it'll fool the detector.'

'That's not so hard,' said Amber.

'It's a lot more difficult than it sounds,' said Hex. 'See how high on the wall the motion-detector is? There's no way to reach it except by climbing up onto the bench. Think about it, Amber. Could you haul yourself up onto the bench, making sure you don't move any part of your body more than two centimetres a minute? I couldn't.'

'I could, though,' said Li.

Alex, Hex and Amber watched in the angled wing mirror as Li glided towards the motion-detector, sliding her bare feet across the kitchen floor a millimetre at a time. She had pushed her long hair down the back of her T-shirt and the can of foam polish was tied securely to her belt. Li reached the bench and slowly, slowly tipped her head up, then down, judging the best way to climb up to the motion detector. She made her decision. Placing her hands on the bench, she lifted her left leg out to the side, slowly raising it higher and higher. The strain showed on her face, but her leg rose smoothly through the air without a single muscle tremor.

'How does she do that?' breathed Hex.

'The muscle strength comes from years of free climbing,' whispered Alex, watching Li in the mirror admiringly. 'And the balance—'

'That'll be the martial arts,' finished Amber.

Li eased her left leg onto the bench top and slid her knee forward until it was in the position she wanted. She rested for a few seconds, then braced herself on her arms and lifted herself slowly upwards until she could slide her left hip onto the bench. Then she began the long task of easing her right leg up behind her. Her arms were quivering with muscle tremors and her face was screwed up in pain by the time she was finally able to lie belly-down on the bench and take the weight off her hands.

Out in the garage, Amber, Hex and Alex breathed a collective sigh of relief. The most difficult part was over. Minutes later, Li was standing on the bench with her back against the kitchen wall. The motion-detector was just above her head.

'Am I out of the beam, Hex?' she asked softly.

Hex studied her position in the mirror. 'You should be.'

Li took a deep breath and yanked the aerosol from her belt. In one smooth movement she reached above her head, pointed the nozzle at the little white box on the wall and pressed down on the top. A stream of creamy white foam smothered the motion-detector.

For a few seconds they all held their breath, but the alarm system stayed quiet. Li reached out and waved her arm up and down in front of the foam-covered detector.

'She did it!' hissed Amber.

Li jumped down from the bench and the other three ran into the kitchen. Alex switched the key to the kitchen side of the connecting door, then softly closed and locked it, just to make sure no-one could walk in on them unannounced. Hex went straight for the laptop while Alex and Amber began to search the drawers and cupboards.

'Empty, empty, empty,' said Amber, moving along the line of drawers.

'Same here,' frowned Alex, opening one cupboard door after another. 'Look, there aren't even any shelves in them. And the fridge isn't plugged in. What's going on?'

There was a serving hatch in the wall. Li gripped the handle at the top of the hatch and slowly eased it open enough for her to peer through to the next room. 'There's nothing in there either,' she whispered. 'Not even a carpet. The place is completely bare.'

Amber was bending down and peering through the keyhole of the door which led from the kitchen to the rest of the house. 'Empty hallway,' she reported. 'Front door at the other end. Staircase . . .' She straightened. 'Perhaps we might find something upstairs.'

'I don't think so,' murmured Alex, remembering something his father had said. 'Not exactly the house of a general, is it?'

'What do you mean?' asked Li.

'This is not his house,' said Alex.

'We broke into the wrong house?' hissed Amber, looking nervously about her.

'No. This house belongs to him,' said Alex. 'But what I mean is, he doesn't live here. It's just a front. Part of the pretence. My guess is that the general has a much grander place somewhere else.'

Li groaned as she rubbed her aching arms. 'Then this has all been a waste of time.'

'Oh, I don't know about that,' said Hex, staring at the laptop screen. 'Come and look.'

They crowded around Hex, peering at the screen over his hunched shoulders. Hex had opened the favourites list on the general's internet explorer utility.

'What are we looking at?' asked Alex.

In answer, Hex moved the mouse pointer to one of the sites on the list. 'It's a Swiss bank,' he said. 'I think that's where he's storing all his funds.'

'Can we get into it?' asked Li.

'First we have to get online, and it's password-protected,' explained Hex.

'Can you crack it?' asked Amber.

'Probably,' said Hex. 'He may be a general in the military sense, but in my world he's only a civilian.'

'If a hacker calls you a civilian, it's like an insult,' explained Amber. 'Civilian is the hacker name for ordinary computer-users.'

'You mean idiots,' muttered Hex. 'Most civilians are idiots – and they have stupid passwords. They're usually only eight characters long, without a single number, only letters.' Hex laughed. 'The stupidest even have an actual word! Can you believe that?'

Alex, Li and Amber laughed with Hex, but shared an embarrassed glance behind his back. They were thinking of their computer passwords – all three of them used real words.

'Real words are easy to remember,' continued Hex, 'but they're also easy to guess.' He laced his fingers together and bent them until the joints cracked, then held his hands poised over the keys. 'All his sites are in English, so I'm guessing his internet access password is in English too.'

Alex nodded, thinking back to his dinner with the general. 'That makes sense. He's very Americanized – and proud of how well he speaks the language.'

Hex typed in PASSWORD. The system rejected it.

He grunted in disappointment. 'You'd be surprised how many civilians use that one,' he explained.

Next, he tried GENERAL. The system rejected it. Hex frowned and tried QUITOLUIS. Again, it was rejected. 'Trouble is, I don't know much about the guy,' sighed Hex. Then he sat up straighter as another idea came to him. He typed in RAT-CATCHER and clicked CONNECT. This time, the system whirred into life. Hex grinned. 'Told you,' he said. 'Computer-users are stupid.'

Less than a minute later the Swiss bank was inviting him to enter his password. 'People tend to use the same password for everything,' muttered Hex. 'I'll try RAT-CATCHER again.' He typed in the word, then cursed as the bank rejected it.

'Well, just keep trying different words,' said Amber.

'Can't,' muttered Hex. 'The bank's security system only allows for three tries, then it gets suspicious. I need to get a tool.'

'From the garage?' asked Amber.

Hex smiled. 'Not that sort of tool,' he said as he began typing furiously. 'I need one of my own software programs. I wrote it to crack passwords.'

'How are you going to get hold of that?' asked Alex.

'I'm downloading it now. I've got stuff stored on other computers all over the place,' explained Hex. 'Most hackers do it. It's safer than keeping everything on your own computer.'

'But don't the other people mind you using their computers?'

Hex grinned. 'They don't know about it. I access big computers with lots of space and lots of users. University computers are the best because their security is so low.'

'Sheesh!' said Amber. 'So you just hack in, dump your stuff and leave?'

'Until I need it. Then I nip back and download it,' said Hex. He pressed a final key and then leaned against the bench, watching the screen. 'There. My program's working on cracking the password now.'

'How long will it take?'

Hex shrugged. 'If it's another proper word, in English, then not long.'

It took less than ten minutes for Hex's program to crack the password.

'Very impressive, Hex!' said Alex.

Hex smiled smugly. 'I got lucky, that's all. It could just as well have taken hours.'

'POWDERKEG?' said Amber, reading the screen. 'What sort of a password is that?'

'It's a small barrel for storing gunpowder, isn't it?' asked Alex.

'Yeah, but "powder" is also a street word for cocaine,' said Hex, as he typed in the password. 'And a keg could be used to store other things. Like money, for instance.'

'So, this account must be where he stores all his drugs money. Pretty good, code-boy,' said Amber grudgingly.

'There it is,' said Hex.

Alex gave a low whistle as he stared at the figures coming up on the screen. General Manteca had millions of dollars stashed away in the bank.

'What are you doing?' asked Li, as Hex began typing again.

'I'm arranging a transfer of funds,' said Hex. 'The general is about to make a very large donation to charity. Any ideas?'

'Yes,' grinned Alex. 'What about Sister Catherine's House? With all that money, she could set up schools and houses for street kids all over Quito.'

Li nodded enthusiastically. 'And university places or job training for the older ones.'

'It's perfect,' agreed Amber. 'The Rat-catcher's funds going to help street kids.'

Hex nodded and dived back into the net, collecting all the details he needed to make a donation to Sister Catherine's House. 'Here we go,' he said, pressing the key that authorized the bank to go ahead with the transfer. 'Now we just need to wait—'

Hex stopped talking and they all froze in place.

Someone had just slotted a key into the front door at the other end of the hallway.

THIRTEEN

'Quick! We have to hide!' hissed Amber, her eyes wild with panic as the key turned and the front door creaked open.

'Where?' whispered Li. Someone stepped into the hallway and closed the front door. A key ring jingled loudly in the silence.

'Cupboards,' whispered Alex, suddenly remembering the empty spaces behind the doors. Li, Amber and Alex each dived for a cupboard and squeezed themselves into the coffin-like spaces beyond. Hex stayed where he was, watching the laptop screen.

'Hex!' breathed Alex, peering out through the latticework of the cupboard door. 'Hide!'

Hex shook his head. His face was pale with fear but also determined. He knew that if he broke the net connection before the transfer was complete, then all his work would be wasted. He turned back to the screen.

Out in the hallway the burglar alarm beeped four times as the security code was punched in. Then footsteps clunked along the bare boards of the hallway, heading for the kitchen door.

'Come on, come on . . .' breathed Hex. His hand was gripping the top of the screen, ready to close the lid as soon as the transfer was complete. The footsteps stopped outside the kitchen door and Hex felt sweat break out on his forehead. He looked back at the screen and there it was, confirmation that the transfer of funds was complete.

Hex slammed the lid down, which automatically severed the internet connection and shut down the laptop, then he dived for the nearest cupboard as the handle of the kitchen door began to turn. Frantically Hex forced himself into the cupboard and tried to shut the door, but it would not close. One of his feet was still poking out over the plinth at the bottom of the cupboard. Hex glanced up. The kitchen door was opening and he was still in full view. Biting his lip against the pain, he grabbed his foot and pulled it until the ankle joint was bent at an impossible angle. With a final twist, his boot slid over the plinth and down into the cupboard. His cupboard door swung shut an instant before General Manteca stepped into the little kitchen.

The four of them froze, cowering in the darkness behind the latticework doors and trying to breathe as shallowly as possible. Hex was in a great deal of pain from his squashed ankle, but he dared not move. They watched through the latticework as the general disconnected the laptop from the wall and shoved it into its carrying case. Alex stared out at the general's face and wondered how he could ever have liked him. Now all the smiles and pretence were gone, he could see a hardness in the man's jawline and a cruel set to the mouth. The general picked up the case, then walked over to the door that connected to the garage. They all tensed. If the general went through into the garage, he would see the broken wing mirror.

The general grabbed the door handle, tested the lock, then nodded and turned away again. Alex sagged with relief, thankful that he had locked the door earlier. The general headed towards the hallway with the laptop. He opened the kitchen door and was about to leave when, somewhere in the room, a cellphone began to ring. Alex jumped at the noise, then clenched his fists. He could not tell where the ringing was coming from. Was it the general's phone, or had Amber's uncle chosen this moment to call her about the satellite images?

The general stopped and stepped back into the room. He put the case down and reached into his pocket. Would he pull out a cellphone or a gun? Alex got ready to burst from the cupboard. If a gun came out he was planning to knock the general to the floor. That way they might have a chance of escaping into the street before he could shoot them. The ringing tone grew louder as the general pulled a phone from his jacket. For the second time in less than a minute, Alex sagged with relief inside the cupboard.

'Manteca,' said the general, leaning back against the bench to take the call. Something made Amber look up at the motion-detector directly above the general's head. Her eyes widened. The blob of foam polish that had been covering the detector was slowly slipping down the front of the little box and forming into a trembling white teardrop hanging from the bottom edge. The drip looked ready to fall at any second. Amber nearly groaned out loud.

'Ross!' said the general. 'Thanks for getting back. Listen, don't go to meet the kids at the airport. They aren't going to make it this time. They're . . . unwell. But don't worry, I have other ways of getting those parcels to you. Do you understand? Good. I'll be in touch.'

The general flicked the phone shut and remained leaning against the bench, deep in thought. Above his head the trembling teardrop grew bigger as more foam slipped over the edge of the detector box. The general flipped the phone open again, then changed his mind and straightened up, just as the foam blob finally began to fall. The general bent to pick up the laptop case and the foam hit the bench behind him with a soft splat. He straightened up and headed out into the hallway, closing the kitchen door behind him.

A few seconds later the alarm system began sounding a muted warning tone, then the front door was pulled shut. The general was gone. Alex, Li and Amber burst out of their cupboards and headed for the door into the garage, with Hex limping along behind them. They tumbled into the garage and pulled the kitchen door shut just as the house alarm finished setting itself and the warning tone stopped.

'When he was talking about the kids, he meant Paulo and Eliza, didn't he?' said Li a few minutes later, as they walked towards the city centre.

'Yes,' said Amber, 'I think so.'

'What did he mean "the kids are . . . unwell"?' demanded Li. 'What has he done to them?'

'Li,' said Hex, 'I know you're worried about Paulo. We all are. But will you stop asking questions we can't answer?'

'Sorry,' muttered Li.

They tramped on in silence for a while, then Li began to talk again, her voice high with anxiety. 'But what if he's hurt really badly? What if we don't get to him in time? I'd never forgive myself if . . . Look, maybe we should tell the authorities – the police, or the army?'

'No, we're on our own,' said Alex. 'We don't know how far the general's influence goes. If we talk to someone in authority here and they turn out to be working with him, then we've just blown our only chance of reaching Paulo and Eliza.'

'But he can't have corrupted the whole army,' insisted Li. 'There must be someone—'

'And how do we know who to trust?' interrupted Alex. 'Like my dad said, the general's men would do anything for him. And if they don't,' he added, remembering the two bodies at the truck stop, 'then he kills them.'

'What about your dad, then?' demanded Li. 'Can he help?'

Alex came to a sudden stop. He had been so busy worrying about Paulo, he had forgotten about his father. 'I have to warn my dad,' said Alex, pulling his cellphone from his pocket. 'I have to warn him about the general. But what can I say? I'm supposed to be in Argentina with Paulo.'

'OK,' said Amber. 'Call to tell him you arrived safely. Then . . . um . . .'

'Does he trust your judgement?' asked Hex.

'Yeah, I think so.'

'Then tell him you didn't like the general,' said Hex. 'Tell him you think he was too good to be true – something like that.'

Alex nodded as he keyed in the number of his father's cellphone. It was a good plan. Planting a doubt about the general in his dad's mind might be all that was needed. The ringing tone was replaced with a click as the call connected.

'Dad!' said Alex. 'I was just calling to say—'

'Hello, Alex,' said a familiar voice. 'Luis Manteca here.'

Alex felt his blood turn to ice. His mouth opened, but no words came out.

The general laughed softly in his ear. 'Alex,' he chided, 'you weren't expecting your father to answer, were you? You know you cannot talk to him.'

'Why not?'

'Have you forgotten? Your father is deep undercover. He cannot be contacted. He left his phone with me.'

'Oh, right,' said Alex, thinking furiously. 'Um, I was just calling to let him know I've arrived safely in Argentina.'

'I will let him know when he gets back to Quito,' said the general.

'When will that be?'

'I have no idea,' said the general. 'Now you must excuse me, Alex. I have to go.'

'Where are you going?' asked Alex, hoping for a clue to help him find Paulo.

'Hunting,' laughed the general. 'I am going hunting.'

The general hung up and Alex was left staring at the puzzled faces of the others as they gathered around him.

'Who were you talking to?' asked Hex.

'General Manteca.'

'What!'

'He said he was going hunting.'

They all stared at one another, trying to guess what the general meant. Then Amber jumped as her own phone started to ring.

'Uncle? You've got the satellite photos? He's where?

OK. We'll meet you at the shop.' Amber disconnected her phone and smiled at the others. 'The satellite located the tracker signal. Paulo's up in the mountains, in some sort of prefabricated building on the edge of a glacier. My uncle reckons it must be the cocaine factory. We're meeting my uncle at the climbing supplies shop in the city centre, to get kitted out. Then we're going in after Paulo and Eliza.'

'At last!' grinned Li. Then her smile disappeared as two pairs of hands grabbed her from behind. The others barely had time to register what was happening before they were grabbed too and twisted round to face a grinning Leo.

Li kicked and struggled, trying to break free, but two more street kids moved in and held her still. 'What does he want?' she gasped, wincing as her wrist was twisted back.

'Revenge,' said Hex grimly, glancing up and down the road. Apart from the four of them and a gang of about sixteen street kids, the road was empty.

Alex opened his mouth and yelled at the top of his voice. 'Help! Somebody help us!' His cries were cut off as a very dirty hand was pressed over his mouth, mashing his lips against his teeth. He twisted his head, trying to see whether anyone was coming. The street remained deserted.

Leo grinned and walked towards Li, who started struggling even harder. 'We have to go find Paulo!' she shouted. 'We don't have time to hang around here while this idiot tries to look big in front of his mates! We—'

Li's head snapped to the side as Leo back-handed her hard across the face. She turned her head back and spat at him.

'*In front of his mates,*' repeated Amber in a dazed voice as she watched the knife appear in Leo's hand. She forced herself to focus on the story she had heard Eliza tell Paulo. There was something in that story Leo would not want her to repeat in front of his friends. Amber's eyes brightened as she remembered. Yes! That was it!

Alex and Hex were both yelling at Leo, warning him not to touch Li.

'Shut up!' shouted Amber. 'Leave this to me.'

Amber began talking to Leo in halting Spanish.

'Good odds, Leo. Sixteen of you against four of us. That tells me one thing about you. You're a coward. I know another thing about you, too.'

Leo frowned and turned towards her, the knife still in his hand. The two boys holding her gripped her arms more tightly as Leo walked towards her.

'I know what you did to Eliza and her brother,' continued Amber hastily. Leo stopped. 'Send your friends away, Leo. I want to talk to you alone. Send them away, or I'll tell them what you did to Eliza.'

Leo sneered at Amber and turned back to Li. The knife glinted in the sun as he lifted it towards her face. Li closed her eyes. Amber thought furiously. OK. So Leo did not mind his friends knowing he was a scumbag. But what if she threatened to tell them something which would isolate Leo from all the other street kids?

'Wait!' shouted Amber desperately. 'If you do that, I'll tell your friends who else was in the alleyway that night. And – I'll tell them you saw him!'

A look of shock appeared on Leo's face. 'Be quiet!' he hissed.

'You want me to say his name now?' asked Amber. 'If you hurt any of us, I promise you, I will say it. I'll tell your friends you saw him that night, unless you make them go away. Now!'

Leo glared at her. He knew that, if the other street kids thought he had seen the face of the Rat-catcher, he would be on his own. A kid alone on the streets of Quito would not last long. Like any true survivor, Leo knew when to retreat. He lowered his knife, then barked orders at the other street kids.

Amber turned to Li, Alex and Hex. 'Stay still,' she ordered in English as the street kids let them go. 'Still and quiet. OK?'

They nodded and Amber turned back to Leo as the other street kids moved off to the end of the street. She talked to him earnestly in Spanish for a few more minutes. Leo scowled as he listened, watching Amber suspiciously and snapping a few short replies. Finally he gave a reluctant nod before he loped off down the street to join the other street kids.

'Come on,' said Amber to the other three. 'Let's get out of here.' She turned and jogged away in the other direction.

'Thanks, Amber,' said Li, catching the other girl up. 'I think you just stopped him playing noughts and crosses on my face.'

'I did more than that,' smiled Amber smugly.

'What did you do?' asked Alex, glancing back over his shoulder to make sure that the street kids weren't following them.

'I persuaded Leo to help us,' said Amber.

'Out of the kindness of his heart?' asked Hex.

'No. I blackmailed him,' grinned Amber.

'But how could he help us?' asked Li.

'He says he knows the gringo soldier with blond hair and grey eyes,' said Amber. 'The one who always gives money to the street kids.'

'Does he mean my dad?' asked Alex.

Amber nodded. 'Leo promised me that he will try to warn the gringo soldier about the general, as soon as the unit comes back to Quito.'

'You don't really think he'll do it, do you?' asked Hex cynically.

Amber shrugged as they jogged on towards the climbing supplies shop. 'Who knows?' she said.

FOURTEEN

'That's a cocaine factory?' cried Amber, staring down at the black and white satellite photograph in disbelief. She was looking at two tiny, battered, prefabricated huts, which were clinging to a large flat rock on the edge of a glacier. 'It's pathetic!'

'What were you expecting, Amber?' asked Hex. 'A big, bright industrial unit with a neon COCAINE FACTORY sign on the front?'

Amber made a face at Hex, then turned to look out of the front windscreen of the van. She glanced down at the map on her lap. 'Next left,' she called, and John Middleton turned the van off the main road onto a rutted, dirt track.

''Fraid it's gonna be like this the rest of the way,' said Amber, as the van bounced and shook, making slow progress up the lower slopes of the mountain. 'We can take the van along to the end of this track, but we have to walk from there.'

It was mid-afternoon. They had been on the road for nearly an hour and most of that time had been spent sorting, stowing or getting into the piles of gear that they had picked up in the climbing supplies shop. They were all kitted out in climbing boots and socks and they were wearing thermal tops and bottoms beneath breathable waterproof jackets and trousers. One hundred per cent UV-proof, wraparound glacier glasses hung from their necks and their faces and hands were smeared with high-factor sun cream. At this altitude, so near the equator, the ultraviolet light was extraordinarily strong, even on overcast days. Once they were above the snow line the risk of severe sunburn would be even greater. The power of the equatorial sun reflecting off snow could burn unprotected skin under the chin, behind the ears and even inside the nostrils. The glacier glasses were essential. Without their protection, it would take as little as fifteen minutes for the ultraviolet light to fry their retinas, causing severe snow-blindness to set in.

There were four rucksacks resting against the back wall of the van, packed with fleece jackets, balaclavas and thick waterproof gloves for the higher slopes, including spares of everything for Paulo and Eliza. Each rucksack was festooned with equipment. There were ice axes, coils of rope and pairs of twelve-point crampons to attach to the soles of their boots once they reached the glacier. A thick sleeping bag, rolled up in a waterproof bivvy bag, was tied to the bottom of each rucksack frame.

The cost of all the equipment had come to thousands of dollars, but John Middleton had paid the overjoyed shop owner without batting an eye. Li had been anxious to get going right away, but the others had insisted on wolfing down a quick pasta meal before they left Quito, to give them energy for the climb. Li had agreed only because she knew Amber had to eat regular meals in order to keep her diabetes under control. Now they were so close to reaching Paulo, Li was nearly bursting with impatience. Ignoring the bone-shaking bumps as the van careered along the rutted track, she frowned down at the satellite photograph, planning their route over and over again.

Alex watched her anxiously. They were all very worried about Paulo, but Li was the closest of them all to the big, gentle Argentinian boy, and Alex was beginning to get concerned about her state of mind. 'How are you doing, Li?' he asked.

'Fine,' muttered Li, flipping him away with an impatient hand. She leafed through a book of climbing routes until she found the right page, then she laid the open book on top of the satellite photograph. 'General Manteca chose his site well,' she said. 'The factory can't be seen from the air except from directly overhead, because it's hidden away at the base of that rock spur, see? And no-one's going to bother to climb up to that particular spot.'

'Why not?' asked Alex.

'There's nothing to attract an experienced mountain-climber. The route up to the glacier is too easy. It's only classed as a Grade One climb. More of a tough walk, really. And any tourists wanting an easy climb-up-to-a-glacier experience are going to head for the bigger, well-known ones, where you get spectacular views and a cup of coffee once you reach the top. There are no views at all from this glacier, because it's hemmed in by bigger mountains on all sides. It's not worth the climb, basically.'

'What about our route, Li?' asked Alex. 'Any danger of us being spotted?'

Li shook her head as she studied the route book and the satellite photograph. 'I don't think so. See how the glacier splits into two forks near the top to pass round each side of that big spur of rock? The cocaine factory is at the base of the rock just there, at the top of the right-hand glacier fork. If we head up the left-hand fork, we'll be hidden by the rock spur. They won't be able to see us.'

'How the hell did the general get those huts up there?' asked Hex, peering over Li's shoulder.

'Easy,' said Alex. 'He has the hardware of the Ecuadorian army at his disposal. My guess is he had the huts flown up there, on cradles, hanging from army helicopters. And look there. See that?' Alex pointed to the side of one of the huts. 'Those five drums? I think that's the consignment of sulphuric acid the general was supposed to be tracking. He probably had them flown in the same way.' Alex shook his head at the sheer nerve of the man.

'That must be the plane that took off from Quito airport with Paulo and Eliza,' said Hex, pointing to a small Dakota at the top edge of the glacier. 'Isn't that dangerous?' he asked. 'Trying to land on ice?'

Amber shook her head. 'No – see, I know about that. I landed on a glacier once, with my mom and dad. We were on vacation in New Zealand. What they do is they bring the plane in to land pointing up the glacier slope and they take off down the glacier slope. See those marks in the snow on the satellite photograph? They're splashes of red-rhodamine dye, put down to mark out the landing strip. There's even a little caterpillar snowplough parked between the huts, see? That's to keep the landing strip clear of soft snow.'

They reached the end of the track a few minutes later and Li slid the side door open while the van was still slowing to a stop. She jumped out and stared up at the mountain. Directly ahead of them were the rich, green pastures of the lower slopes. They gradually changed to the bleak, high-altitude grasslands known as the páramo. The snow line cut horizontally across the top edge of the páramo slopes as though someone had drawn a line with a ruler, and above the snow line was the glacier and rock landscape of the summit. Li stared up at the stark, black rock outcrop which stood out against the white of the glacier. Paulo was in a hut on the other side of that rock outcrop, and she was going to rescue him, whatever it took.

Li shouldered her rucksack and set off up the mountain at a blistering pace, leaving the others scrambling to catch up with her.

'Wait!' called John Middleton.

Amber sighed. 'I knew it. When it comes down to it, he's scared to let us go off alone.'

Reluctantly, Li stopped and Amber hurried back down the slope to her uncle, followed by Hex.

'Sweetheart,' said John Middleton. 'I'm really not sure about this—'

'Listen to me, Uncle,' said Amber, firmly. 'We have to go get Paulo. You can't stop us now.'

'Then I should've stopped it earlier,' said John Middleton.

'You couldn't've stopped us,' said Hex, flatly. 'Alpha Force would've happened whether you wanted it to or not.'

'Maybe I should come with you—'

Amber giggled and poked the middle-aged paunch around her uncle's belly. 'You? Mountain-climbing? No way! Stick to what you're good at. You make a really great anchor man. Things would've been a lot tougher without you.'

'But, to let a bunch of kids go into danger—'

'You want to talk about danger?' said Amber, suddenly serious. 'If it wasn't for Alpha Force, I wouldn't be here now. In the year after Mom and Dad died, I was admitted to hospital four times with hypos and suchlike. You know why? Because I didn't care. I didn't care about my life enough to manage my diabetes. Since we started Alpha Force, I've been fine. I have a reason to care now – and I feel closer to Mom and Dad. We can do this, Uncle. Really, we can.'

John Middleton sighed, then reached out and cupped Amber's face in his hands. 'OK,' he said.

Amber grinned and gave her uncle a quick kiss on the cheek, then she and Hex hurried back up the slope to join Li and Alex.

'Be careful,' called John Middleton. 'Remember everything you've learned in training! And keep in touch!'

Amber waved her cellphone at him. 'Every six hours,' she promised. 'See you back here, Uncle.'

'I'll be waiting,' said John Middleton gruffly, folding his arms and blinking rather more than was necessary.

For the first few hours the going was easy. They trekked up the lower slopes, past terraced fields full of flowers. Hummingbirds darted everywhere in a bright blur of feathers, dipping their long beaks into the flower heads. The sun was warm and the grass in the paddocks was a rich green. There were flocks of sheep there, and an occasional belching llama, standing head and shoulders above the milling flock and watching them with big, soulful eyes. As they walked, Alex picked up dry twigs and sticks along the way and pushed them into the side pocket of his rucksack.

'Force of habit,' he grinned, when the others looked at him in bewilderment.

Gradually the slopes steepened as they climbed further up the mountain, and the sprinkling of tiny thatched houses where the mountain farmers lived began to thin out. The flocks of sheep were replaced by goats, roaming freely on the mountainside and tearing hungrily at the spiky, tough grass. Clouds moved in to cover the sun. A cold wind began to blow and the temperature gradually dropped from T-shirt mild to teeth-chattering cold. They had reached the start of the páramo.

'I think I need to stop for a while,' gasped Amber, after they had been climbing through the high-altitude grasslands for two hours. The air had been growing steadily thinner as the altitude increased and they were all having to breathe faster in order to force enough oxygen into their blood, but Amber seemed to be suffering more than the rest of them.

'Just a bit further,' said Li, without turning round.

'Hang on a minute,' said Hex. He stood in front of Amber, lifted her chin with his fingers and studied her face. There were beads of sweat on her forehead and the skin around her mouth was a sickly-looking grey. 'We're stopping,' he insisted.

'But Paulo is up there,' said Li sharply.

'Five minutes,' said Hex. His voice was calm, but his green eyes were worried as he studied Amber. 'We all need a break.'

Li sighed and headed for a large rock where they could shelter from the freezing wind which was howling down from the higher mountain passes. The spongy, wet ground squelched under them as they sat huddled together and they were glad of the protection of their waterproof trousers.

'Bit of a change from the lower slopes,' said Alex with a shiver, looking around at the grey, brittle landscape. 'I think it's time to put another layer on.'

They all struggled into their fleece jackets, gloves and balaclavas, except Amber. She took out her phone first, and sent a text message to her uncle. Then she pulled her diabetes kit from her belt pouch and did a blood-sugar test.

'Is it OK?' asked Hex, as Amber pulled out her insulin pen.

'It's fine,' said Amber, peeling layers of clothing

away from the top of her thigh and administering her second injection of the day.

'Are you sure?' persisted Hex. 'You're not looking too good.'

'I don't feel great,' admitted Amber, shivering as she pulled on her fleece jacket. 'But I'm not having a hypo. The blood sugar's fine.'

'It's mild altitude sickness,' said Li. 'That's all. We're all suffering a bit because we're climbing so fast.'

'What are the symptoms?' asked Hex, still studying Amber.

'Breathlessness, fast pulse, headaches. Oh, and dehydration. We lose more moisture because we're breathing faster.'

'Time for a drink, then,' said Alex, pulling a bottle of water from his rucksack and handing it round.

'Can we do anything about it?' asked Hex.

'Nope,' said Li, doling out high-calorie snack bars for everyone to chew on. 'The longer we stay this high, the worse the symptoms get. That's why we should push on.'

'OK,' said Amber, struggling to her feet and trying to ignore the wave of dizziness that overtook her. She gazed up at the mountain and her mouth dropped open. 'Would you look at that?'

They all looked up and stared in amazement. A thick grey fog was racing down the mountain towards them, carried on the freezing wind. It moved like a torrent of water, pouring through gullies and swirling over rocks. Within seconds they were enveloped in a bitterly cold, grey blanket and visibility dropped to virtually nothing.

'Well, that's just great,' sighed Amber, reaching into her rucksack and pulling out her compass and a map in a waterproof covering. She studied them for a moment, getting her bearings, then she hung the map and compass around her neck. 'That way,' she said, pointing into the fog.

An hour later, the strengthening wind suddenly tore the fog apart like tissue paper and blasted it away down the slope behind them. They were left standing on the exposed shoulder of the mountain, with clear skies above them and the start of the snow line only a few metres away. The sun had already dipped behind the other side of the mountain and the left fork of the glacier stretched ahead of them like a white highway in the dim late-afternoon light. Over to the right, the dark bulk of the rock outcrop towered over them.

'Good compass work, Amber!' yelled Alex, over the howling wind. 'Spot on!'

Amber nodded and grinned weakly from where she stood, clinging to Hex's arm and gasping for breath.

'Fix the crampons onto your boots now!' shouted Li, once they were out on the face of the glacier. 'And then we need to rope ourselves together before we go any further!'

They nodded, turned their backs to the wind and sat down to fasten the twelve-spiked crampons onto the soles of their boots. Li secured the rope around her waist, then moved from Hex, to Amber, to Alex, knotting the rope around their waists and leaving ten metres of line between each of them. They huddled together while Li gave last-minute instructions. 'Keep the line strung out, OK? It's safer that way. If one of us falls down a crevasse, we don't want the rest of us getting dragged in as well.'

'OK, let's go,' shouted Alex.

Li nodded but hesitated, glancing over her shoulder at the glacier. For the first time since they started the climb, she seemed unsure about carrying on. She walked a few metres, then bent down, took off her glove and picked up a handful of snow with her bare hand.

'What is it, Li?' asked Alex, stomping through the snow to join her.

Li gave him a sideways glance but said nothing.

'Tell me,' said Alex.

'This isn't looking too good,' admitted Li. She held out the handful of snow. 'You know how we had rain last night in Quito? Well, up here, it was falling as snow. Now, this layer of fresh snow has had the sun on it all afternoon.' Li let the snow sift through her fingers. 'See the consistency? Like sugar. That's going to make the climbing hard going and . . .'

'And what?' prompted Amber.

'And it makes an avalanche far more likely,' said Li. She looked down at her boots before she said the next bit. 'You see, climbers usually start out on a short route like this at dawn, so they're back down again before noon. Before the sun has had a chance to warm the snow. But — we're crossing this glacier at the most dangerous time of day.'

'And you wait until we're up here before you tell us this?' snarled Hex.

Li's head snapped up and she glared at him. 'Why? Would it have made any difference if I'd told you at the bottom?'

'At least we'd have had a choice in the matter!'

'Paulo is up there!' hissed Li. 'Would you have chosen to wait until tomorrow morning?'

Hex stared at her for a moment, his jaw clenching and unclenching. Then his shoulders relaxed and he shook his head. 'No.'

Li looked at Alex, then at Amber. They both shook their heads. 'OK, then,' said Li. 'Remember what I said, keep the line strung out.'

The night drew in, the wind yowled and the air grew colder as they moved up the glacier slope. Li led the way and they tramped along behind her, strung out in a long line in the powdery snow. The moon rose behind them and their long black shadows walked across the luminous face of the glacier beside them. Amber stumbled along in a daze, her head spinning and her breath coming in frantic gasps. Hex kept stopping and sending worried glances over his shoulder at her, but then the rope around his waist would tug as Li ploughed on up the slope and he would have to start moving again.

Suddenly, Hex felt the rope go slack in front of him. Li had stopped. She was standing, staring at the surface of the glacier ahead. Hex looked back at Alex, who shrugged. Amber did not even raise her head to see what was happening. She just stood there with her head down. Alex hesitated, remembering Li's instructions to stay apart, but Li stayed motionless, staring at the snow. Alex went to Amber and helped her up the slope to Hex, then the three of them moved up to join Li.

Alex pulled his balaclava away from his mouth. 'What's up?' he yelled, turning his back to the wind.

'Snow bowl,' said Li briefly. 'See it?'

Hex stared out at the glacier and shrugged. It all looked the same to him.

'The colour's different. And see how it's slightly curved, like a pillow? It was once a hollow in the surface of the glacier, but it's filled up with layers of packed snow.'

'So what's the problem?' asked Alex.

'Could be unstable,' said Li.

'What about going round it?'

'That would make the climb longer,' said Li. 'If we keep going straight on, we could be at the glacier fork in just over an hour!'

Alex looked at her. 'It's your call,' he said. 'But remember, we can't rescue Paulo if we're dead.'

Li did not return his grin. Her face was serious as she studied the snow. 'We go on,' she decided. 'There's been no sign of danger so far.'

They spread out again and continued on their way, heads down against the wind. Li was well onto the snow bowl and Alex had just walked over the rim, when a deep, regular booming began to sound, as though someone was beating a very large drum. Li and Alex stopped instantly, but Hex tramped on for a few more steps, pulling Amber along behind him, before he realized that the booming noise matched his steps. It was the packed snow beneath his feet that was resonating hollowly, every time his boots struck it.

Hex looked up at Li. She had turned to face them and her normally rosy high cheekbones were as pale as candlewax in the moonlight. Hex felt a bolt of fear slam into him as he stared at Li's terrified face. For a few seconds they stood, frozen. Then, with a muffled *whoomp,* a whole section of the glacier surface over to their left shook and settled as though all the air had been knocked out of it.

Li froze, watching the snow. She knew that a weaker, older layer of snow had just collapsed under the slab of snow to their left. It was now extremely unstable and could quite easily slide off the glacier like a plate from a tilting table. If that happened, they would be taken down the mountain with the avalanche. She waited for a few seconds, then decided to retrace her steps. As soon as she put her foot down, cracks appeared in the snow, spreading outward from under her boot in a star pattern. Li felt her mouth go dry. Snow only cracked like that when it was under great pressure. The slab they were standing on was about to collapse.

FIFTEEN

Li took a deep breath and looked up at the others. They were all watching her, waiting to know what to do. She pointed towards the rock outcrop at the right-hand edge of the glacier, then slowly started to move towards it, away from the unstable slabs of snow to their left. With every step she took, the snow slab boomed and a spiderweb of cracks spread away from her boots, but there was no option. They had to move out of the snow bowl and hope that they made it before the slabs detached themselves from the glacier and avalanched down the mountain.

The minutes ticked by as they crawled across the glacier towards the rock outcrop. Finally they reached snow that did not boom like a drum when they stepped on it, but they were still in great danger. Li could not understand why the unstable slabs had not avalanched already. The relatively shallow angle of the slope and the steadily dropping temperature must have kept them in place, but that could not last much longer. They had to climb higher, round the edge of the snow bowl, so that they were above the avalanche when it happened.

Li pulled a snow stake from her rucksack and moved off up the slope, probing the snow as she went. The snow here was less unstable because it had been in the shade of the rock outcrop all day, but she knew they faced another problem. When a glacier came up against rock like this outcrop, deep crevasses could open up along the edge of the glacier, hidden under layers of snow.

They were barely clear of the snow bowl when there was an explosive crack and the slabs behind them finally began to slide, picking up speed as they moved down the slope until they were roaring down the mountain at the speed of an express train, sending huge clouds of powdered snow into the air and taking massive boulders bouncing down the mountain with them. Alex, Li, Hex and Amber watched from the safety of the rock outcrop, each imagining what could have happened.

'Sorry,' said Li, as the rumbling died away down the mountain.

'We survived,' said Alex, 'but is it safe to go on?'

'Oh, yes,' said Li, turning away rather too quickly.

The other three looked at one another, then turned to follow her. They were all panting hard now, but they made good progress, following the rock outcrop. When Li stopped for a breather, Alex raised his head to look up the moonlit slope. He thought he could just see the top end of the rock outcrop in the distance. Paulo and Eliza were just round the other side of that outcrop. Alex felt his heart lift but, at the same time, the metallic taste of fear came into his mouth at the thought of what they were about to do.

Ahead of him, Li started out again. Alex took a step forward – and the ground opened up under his feet. There was a brief, dizzy sensation of falling into darkness, then he was jerked to a halt by the rope around his waist. He swung on the end of the rope, gasping with shock and pain. He tried to straighten up and grab the rope to stop it from biting into him. The rope slid up around his chest and began to constrict his already overworked lungs. Alex hung in the intense coldness of the crevasse, gasping for air. He peered up at the faint glow of moonlight far above his head until a grey mist came down over his eyes and his head lolled back.

Up on the surface of the glacier, Amber screamed as the rope jerked her from her feet. She slid down the slope on her back, heading for the black crevasse that had opened up in the white snow. Behind her, Hex lost his footing too. 'Li!' he bellowed as he slid.

Li jammed her crampons into the snow and leaned back against the rope. Below her, Hex stabbed at the snow with the spikes of his crampons, gradually slowing his downward slide. Li pulled the ice axe from her belt, slipped the strap around her wrist and slammed it into the slope above her. She hung on with both hands. The rope jerked, nearly pulling her arms from their sockets. Hex dug his crampons in deep and took hold of the rope too. His arms strained as he hauled back on the rope and, finally, Amber came to a floundering halt on the lip of the crevasse.

'Amber!' called Li, her voice wobbling with strain. 'Can you move up the slope at all?'

Amber turned onto her back, grabbed the rope and began to dig her crampons into the snow. Above her, Li and Hex did the same and, gradually, they moved up the slope in a series of short, grunting heaves.

'OK! Stop!' yelled Li, when she judged that Amber was out of danger. 'Alex? Can you hear us?'

There was no answer. Li groaned, trying to decide what to do. 'Hex and Amber? Do you think you can take the strain?'

Hex dug his crampons in deeper and hauled back on the rope. Below him, Amber took her ice pick from her belt and anchored herself to the snow. Li felt her section of rope slacken. Carefully, she got to her feet and hurried down the slope to Hex, untying the rope around her waist as she went.

'I think Alex must've passed out because of the rope around his chest,' she panted as she reached Hex. 'I'm going to go down there and see.'

'Careful,' grunted Hex, his face taut with strain.

Li edged as close to the crevasse as she dared, pulling another rope from her rucksack as she went. She put a loop in one end of the rope, then measured out a ten-metre length and tied it onto the taut rope that linked Alex and Amber. Li threw the new rope over the edge of the crevasse, then started calling to Alex.

Down in the crevasse, Alex swam up out of a cold, grey mist. Someone was shouting to him, but he could not understand the words. He tried to lift his head and the rope tightened around his chest. The pain brought him fully awake again and he heard Li's voice floating down from above him.

'Alex! Put your foot through the loop!'

Alex turned his head and saw the new rope dangling in front of him. He reached out and grabbed it, then slipped his boot into the loop at the bottom. As soon as the new rope took his weight, the rope around his chest slackened and his head began to clear.

'He's done it!' yelled Li, running back up the slope and tying herself back onto the other end of the rope. 'We can pull now. Go!'

They pulled as hard as they could, backing up the slope and digging their crampons in for purchase. Soon, Alex's head appeared. They pulled harder and he slid over the lip of the crevasse onto the snow. Once he was well clear of the crevasse, they helped him to his feet and took him to safety.

'That's it,' growled Alex, as soon as he could talk. 'I'm calling a halt.'

'But we're nearly there!' cried Li.

'Li, you're too tied up with getting to Paulo,' said Alex, rubbing his sore chest. 'Your judgement is way off. If we keep doing as you say, somebody's going to die.'

'He's right, Li,' gasped Amber.

'Let's wait a few hours,' agreed Hex. 'Give the snow time to harden. We can still be there before dawn – sneak in while they're all sleeping.'

Li looked at the three of them, then nodded a reluctant agreement.

'Is there a way of getting out of this wind?' asked Hex, giving Amber a worried look.

Alex looked around until he spotted a promising drift of deep, hardened snow against the rock face. 'Over there,' he said, pulling a snow shovel from his pack. 'We can dig a snow hole.'

They piled their rucksacks around Amber, giving her some shelter from the wind. Alex dug into the snow bank, keeping the entrance small and low to the ground but hollowing out a larger, low-ceilinged space beyond the entrance, inside the bank. Li and Hex cleared away the snow that Alex pushed out through the entrance hole.

Once the space was big enough for all four of them, Alex set about creating three different shelving levels inside. He had built a snow hole with his dad once, out on the Northumbrian moors, and he knew they worked on the principle that hot air rises, and heavier, cold air sinks. The smallest shelf was the highest, where the fire would be. When Alex had finished it, he took Li's snow stake and pushed it carefully up through the roof of the shelter to create a narrow chimney above the fire. Next, he levelled out a second, much larger platform just below the fire platform, for them all to sit on. The third level was a small trench dug just inside the entrance hole and that was where the cold air would gather, leaving the warmer air circulating on the higher platforms. Finally he picked up the block of snow he had kept back from the trench and slotted it into the entrance hole as a door. Nodding with satisfaction, he put the block to one side and crawled out into the freezing wind. The whole process had taken less than half an hour of hard digging.

They all crawled into the snow hole out of the wind and snuggled down into their sleeping bags, which were protected by waterproof bivvy bags. Alex took the sticks he had collected from the lower slopes of the mountain and laid them on the fire shelf. He pulled his survival kit from his belt pouch and took out a twist of tinder-dry kindling and his flint. Within minutes there was a small fire crackling brightly on the fire shelf and the snow hole began to warm up.

Amber sent a text message to her uncle, then they

leaned together, exhausted and panting hard in the thin air, waiting in silence for the dawn.

Hex was right. Even with a few hours of rest, they still made it to the top of the left-hand glacier fork just as the sun was rising. The wind had dropped and the glacier slope below them was quiet as they eased their way around the top of the rock outcrop. They went down on their bellies and commando-crawled down the right-hand fork of the glacier, until they reached a small ridge in the snow.

Carefully, Hex raised his head above the ridge, then signalled the all-clear. The others raised their heads to have a look. The two huts lay directly below them on a rock shelf next to the glacier. The little six-seater Dakota was still poised at the top of the landing strip, with its nose pointing down the glacier. Everything was quiet and still.

Li took the tracker device from her rucksack and pulled out the telescopic aerial. Hex leaned over and turned down the sound before Li switched it on. The green blip appeared on the screen, flashing strongly. Hex peered at the distance and direction statistics coming up in the corner of the screen, then pointed to the furthest away of the two huts. 'He's in that one,' he whispered.

They nodded and retreated a little way up the slope to dump their rucksacks behind a rock and remove their crampons. Amber sent another reassuring text message to her uncle, then turned off the phone and slipped it into her rucksack. Then she quickly gave herself her morning insulin injection.

'Ready?' whispered Alex. 'Let's go get Paulo.'

There were well-worn tracks of packed-down snow all around the huts and they were able to move along them without making a sound. They moved in single file, crouching low to the ground. They reached the first hut and Alex slowly raised his head until he could peer in through the window. There were three camp beds in there, arranged around an oil stove, and three humped shapes on the beds under mounds of blankets.

Alex crouched down again, mimed sleeping and gave a thumbs-up. If things went to plan, they were going to be able to sneak Paulo and Eliza out of the other hut and have them halfway down the left-hand fork of the glacier before the inhabitants of the other hut had even woken up.

They moved on in silent single file through the snow to the second hut. Again, Alex raised his head to look through the window. The sun shone into the room beyond, lighting up a strange collection of large tubs and barrels, with siphon pipes strung between them. They had found the general's cocaine factory. Over in one corner a clump of yellowy, powdery substance had been spread out on a tarpaulin square to dry. There were tables lined up against the back wall. Some were stacked with white blocks wrapped in clingfilm, others held collections of bottles and chemical containers. A large sink stood in another corner, next to a dirty old cooker, which was connected to a Calor Gas bottle. The far corner of the room was screened off with an old blanket, hanging from a length of washing line.

Alex gestured to the other three and they joined him at the window. He pointed to the screened-off corner. 'They must be behind there,' he breathed.

Hex moved up to the door and checked all around it for any sort of alarm system, then he reached out and turned the handle. The door swung open. He frowned suspiciously and turned to Li. 'Why isn't the door locked?'

'They must be tied up,' she whispered, peering into the dark hut. 'Besides, who needs locks on doors way up here?'

Still Hex hesitated. Li pushed past him impatiently and stepped into the hut. The others followed her, closing the door behind them. They moved over to the blanket. Hex and Alex nodded to one another, then reached up, grabbed a corner of the blanket each and yanked it down.

There was nothing but a small table behind the blanket. On top of the table, arranged neatly right in the centre, was Paulo's belt.

'It's a trap!' hissed Amber.

Then the hut door opened behind them. A small cylinder came rolling into the room and the door closed again. Amber, Li and Hex stared stupidly at the cylinder, not understanding what it was, but Alex's eyes widened. He knew what the cylinder was. It was a stun grenade, commonly known as a flash-bang.

'Get down!' he yelled, diving under the table. 'Hands over your ears!'

The others dropped to the floor beside him. An instant later, the stun grenade exploded with a blast of brilliant light and overwhelming sound. The percussion hit them like a solid wall, knocking the wind from their lungs and setting their heads ringing like tuning forks. They flopped onto the floor and their hands fell away from their ears. They stared unseeingly at the ceiling, completely overcome. The pain in their ears was intense and the ringing grew louder and louder, disrupting the delicate balance-mechanism of the inner ear completely. Vertigo gripped them and a huge wave of nausea flowed through their bodies.

They were vaguely aware of being picked up and manhandled out of the hut, but they were so disoriented, they could not even stand. By the time their heads had cleared enough for them to realize what was happening, they were outside, sitting in a line in the snow. Their wrists were handcuffed behind them, and a thin chain had been threaded through each pair of cuffs, then padlocked to the propane gas tank which stood between the huts.

Amber was the last to come round. She leaned over and vomited into the snow, then looked over at the other three, blinking the tears from her eyes. They were glaring up at three men, who stood over them, smiling. Two of them were the adoption men from Quito. The third was a thin, hawk-faced man. Alex recognized him from the truck stop on the border road. He was one of General Manteca's men.

'Amber,' said Alex tightly, 'can you talk to them? Pretend we don't know anything. Tell them we are only climbers who got lost. Tell them we just stumbled onto the huts looking for help—'

'Do not bother,' said the thin-faced man in strongly accented English. 'We know who you are.'

'What have you done with Paulo?' yelled Li.

'Ah,' said the thin-faced man, pretending to be sad. 'He was so brave. I hurt him a lot, but he would not tell us anything. Then the general suggested I should start making little Eliza very uncomfortable – and suddenly, we could not shut Paulo up. He told us all about you.' The man sighed. 'Poor Paulo.'

Li began to cry softly.

'Don't worry,' said the man kindly. 'It will all be

over soon. There is an explosive charge on the side of this gas tank, set to go off in ten minutes. You have caused us a lot of trouble, but the trail ends here. You and the factory will . . . disappear, and we will start up a new factory somewhere else. Do you see how you have wasted your last few days on this earth?'

The man turned on his heel and headed for the plane, shouting something in Spanish to the other two. They dived into the hut to get their luggage and the last of the cocaine.

'What are we going to do?' cried Amber, struggling against the handcuffs.

Alex shook his head grimly. He could see the device, stuck to the side of the tank, just above his head. There was enough explosive there to leave nothing but a smoking hole in the mountainside.

The thin-faced man had nearly reached the plane when his cellphone rang. The seconds ticked by as he listened, then he flicked the cellphone shut and walked back to them, pulling out a pistol.

'Change of plan,' he said, aiming the pistol at Amber's head as the other two men piled out of the hut behind him. The two adoption men came closer, grinning and eager to watch. Suddenly the thin-faced man twisted round, holding the gun at eye level. There were two blasts in quick succession. The adoption men staggered backwards with surprised expressions on their faces and round, red holes in the middle of their foreheads. They fell onto the snow and lay still. Their blood seeped into the snow around them in a spreading circle.

Li screamed and screwed her eyes shut as the man turned back to them. He laughed as he unlocked the padlock holding the chain to the tank. 'I told you,' he said as he yanked them to their feet by the chain. 'Change of plan. The general wants to see you – all of you. He has discovered a certain . . . lack of funds. He would like to know where his money has gone.'

They staggered and stumbled over the snow towards the plane, horribly aware of the explosive device ticking away behind them. The thin-faced man pushed them roughly into the passenger compartment of the plane and padlocked the chain linking their handcuffs to a metal strut in the framework, then he climbed into the pilot's seat and started the engine.

The little plane trundled down the glacier slope, picking up speed all the way. The man pulled back on the joystick and the plane left the ground. He yanked it round in a tight turn, making the engines roar, then pointed it straight at the mountainside ahead. Gradually, the little plane climbed, all the while rushing towards the rock face. When it seemed as though they would crash, he pulled the plane into a banking turn which took them towards a narrow gap between the jagged peaks.

A bright orange flower of fire blossomed on the glacier below, followed by a dull crump as the sound of the explosion reached them. The little plane shuddered, buffeted by the turbulence from the explosion. Then they were through the gap between the peaks and flying up into the clear blue morning sky.

SIXTEEN

The general's house was huge and grand – a white, Spanish colonial-style mansion set in grounds that covered many thousands of acres. Cultivated fields and gardens surrounded the house while, further out, the land was covered with forest and lakes. The estate was situated in a remote part of the Central Valley, south-west of Quito. As the plane had circled overhead, preparing to land on the estate's private landing strip, Alex had spotted only one road, stretching away like a long, thin ribbon to the east, where he thought it must eventually join the Pan-American Highway.

Now, as the off-road vehicle ferrying them from the landing strip rolled to a halt on the gravelled circle in front of the mansion, General Manteca hurried down the steps to meet them, like a host coming out to welcome his weekend house-guests.

'Alex!' cried the general as Alex stumbled from the car, followed by Amber, Hex and Li. 'How good to see you again!'

Alex glared at the general, then looked around him. There were two gardeners weeding the driveway and a housemaid moved around on the sunny veranda at the top of the steps, setting a table for breakfast.

'Help us!' yelled Alex. 'Help!'

The gardeners carried on weeding. The housemaid dropped a spoon and hurriedly picked it up again. None of them lifted their heads to look at him.

'They work for me, Alex,' said the general. 'They know when to be deaf and blind. Come. Sit with me on the veranda.'

The general turned away and strolled up the steps. Alex, Li, Amber and Hex looked at one another, wondering whether to make a run for it, but the thin-faced man was getting out of the car behind them and they were still chained together with their arms cuffed behind their backs. Silently, they stumbled up the steps after the general. He waved them to a long, cushioned sofa, which swung gently in its frame as they sat down on it. A gentle breeze from the ceiling fan cooled the air, dappled sunlight made the veranda boards glow and the smell of fresh coffee and bacon filled the air. It was so strange to be sitting in the middle of this peaceful scene, sweating in their layers of mountain gear, with their faces streaked with dirt and their wrists bleeding from the rub of the handcuffs.

The general sat down at the table and the thin-faced man stood a discreet distance away at the top of the steps, with his back to them, as though he was a butler in a stately home rather than a ruthless gunman.

'So,' said the general, helping himself to bacon and eggs. 'Paulo told me all about how angry you were when your father cancelled your holiday, Alex. He told me how you hated being packed off like a little boy, so you called up all your friends here, to help you prove to your father how grown up you are. You thought you could teach him a lesson by beating him at his own game. Am I right?'

Alex nodded, keeping his head down. He dared not meet the general's gaze until he understood exactly what sort of a tale Paulo had spun. It seemed that he had managed to leave Alpha Force out of the story. The general seemed to think it had all been done in a fit of childish temper.

'I understand, Alex,' said General Manteca, 'and I must say, you chose your friends well for your little game. Resourceful – and wealthy too, I imagine. Tracker devices are expensive toys and the one you used must have been state of the art.'

Amber stiffened with hope beside Alex. The general did not know about the satellite images, which suggested that he did not know about her uncle! A second later she slumped again, as she realized that her uncle would not be expecting a call from her for another five hours. Even then, he would have no idea where they were.

'You have done well,' said the general. 'But this was a dangerous game you chose to play, not a bit of harmless fun! And now, look at the position you find yourselves in. You have all lied to your parents, telling them you are staying at one another's houses, so nobody knows where you are.'

General Manteca leaned forward and fixed them with his dark brown eyes. He was trying to look unconcerned, but his hands were gripping his knife and fork so hard, his knuckles were white. 'I will make a deal with you,' he said casually. 'You tell me where my money is and how to get it back. Then I will arrange to have you set free.'

'I can tell you where it is, no problem,' said Hex. 'Yesterday you made a large, anonymous donation to Sister Catherine's House. It's all sitting in the charity's bank account right now. As for getting it back, well, that's a different story. You can't. Get it back, I mean. Still, it must be good to know the Rat-catcher's money will be helping all those street kids.'

The general's breakfast plate flew across the veranda and smashed against the white wall, leaving a yellow and red smear of egg and tomato. A maid scurried out from the house to clear it up.

'Street kids!' roared Luis Manteca, his face red

and twisted with anger. 'Street *rats*, you mean! Lice-ridden, diseased vermin!' He shook his head like an angry bull, then took a deep breath. 'If you think this set-back will stop me, you are very wrong. I can start a new factory tomorrow. And my business is growing all the time. I can replace those funds in less than a year!'

'What have you done with Paulo?' asked Li. 'Have you . . .? Is he . . .?'

'Dead?' The general subsided into his chair again with a cruel smile. 'Not yet. But he soon will be. As will all of you.' He sighed and turned to the thin-faced man. 'I'm growing tired of this,' he said. 'Take them over to the compound.'

'What about my father?' said Alex. 'I left him a message about you, you know.'

'No, Alex, you didn't.' The general pulled a cellphone from his shirt pocket. 'This is his phone. I took the only call you made to him. There are no text messages either. At least, not from you. He did get one this morning, from your mother, in Paris. She was at the top of the Eiffel Tower and she sent a text to say that she was missing you both and wished you were there with her. Wasn't that sweet?'

Alex clenched his jaw and swallowed hard, trying to get rid of the lump in his throat at the unexpected message from his mother.

'Nobody has left any messages at the base either,' continued the general. 'Or at the hotel you and your father stayed in. Your father suspects nothing. When he returns from his wild goose chase around Guayaquil, grieving for his missing son, I, his good friend, will be there to support him. And when your heart-broken father shoots himself in the head a few weeks from now – I already have it marked in my diary – I will cry at his graveside. After that, I can get on with my business undisturbed. Now, if you would like to follow me to the car—'

'Wait! Tell me something first,' said Alex, desperately stalling for time. 'There's something I don't understand. Why use street kids?'

'What do you mean, Alex?'

'Why use street kids to carry drugs for you? You have so much power, you could simply fly the drugs over the border by the planeload, or drive them out in convoys of trucks. Why use kids as mules? They couldn't carry much.'

'What do you think, Alex? Do you have a theory?'

'I'm not sure,' said Alex. 'But I think it has something to do with the Rat-catcher. He hasn't been hunting recently, has he?'

The general nodded. 'You are a bright boy, Alex. I enjoyed hunting as the Rat-catcher for a time, but then I grew bored. The street rats were so plentiful and so easy to find. And there was no sense of danger. The people of Quito did not seem to care about the Rat-catcher. Some of them secretly admired him, I think. None of them tried to stop him. So I retired the Rat-catcher six months ago, and instead I found a way to bring the street rats running to me.'

'The adoption men?' said Amber.

'That's right! And, Alex, once again, you are correct. I did not need to use the street kids as mules. I used them because it amused me to have them take special parcels to my most valued clients — just as it has amused me to play this game with you. And I always gave the little rats exactly what I promised them. They all ended up on a big estate with a grand house and lots of land.'

'You mean here?' guessed Li.

'Exactly,' smiled Luis Manteca.

'What happened to them then?' whispered Amber.

'That is what I want to show you!' said the general, jumping to his feet with boyish enthusiasm. 'I have discovered a much more enjoyable way of hunting rats!'

Paulo came awake in the darkness. His head was swimming with the after-effects of the sleeping drug that had been put in the food. He had no idea where he was or how long he had been asleep. Eliza lay beside him, quiet and still. He reached out and touched her hand. It was icy cold. A thrill of fear ran through him as he felt his way up to her face. What if the drug had been too strong for her? What if she had died in her sleep? He held his hand above her mouth and sagged with relief when he felt the feathery touch of her breath on his palm.

Paulo lay still for a moment, trying to figure out

where they were. The floor beneath them was covered in a thick layer of sawdust. Were they in a stable of some sort? He listened, but there were no swishing tails or friendly whinnies, only a cold, echoing emptiness. Paulo clambered to his feet, groaning at the flaring pains all over his beaten body. He put his arms out in front of him and stumbled forward until he came into contact with a wall. He ran his hands over the wall. It was hard and smooth. It felt like some sort of glass.

Paulo almost screamed as a set of powerful arc lights suddenly clicked on overhead. He fell backwards, away from the wall, shielding his one good eye against the blinding light with his arm. Eliza moaned beside him, then came awake, whimpering as a muffled banging started on the other side of the glass wall.

Paulo forced himself to open his good eye. He squinted through his fingers at the glass wall. Then his mouth dropped open with shock as he saw Li on the other side of the glass, shouting soundlessly and kicking the wall with her boots. Alex was there too, and Amber and Hex. Paulo's face lit up with pleasure for an instant. Then his face fell as he noticed that all four of them were chained together like a bunch of convicts. Behind them stood the general and the thin-faced man who had been such an expert at causing him pain.

'It will not break,' said the general calmly, as Li continued to kick at the glass wall. 'It is strengthened glass, built to withstand . . . Well, you will see what it was built to withstand in just a moment.'

'Paulo!' sobbed Li, watching as he tried to clamber to his feet in the sawdust circle on the other side of the glass. His face was purpled with bruises and one eye was just a swollen, bleeding lump.

'He cannot hear you,' explained the general. 'It is soundproofed.'

'What are you going to do to him?' demanded Hex.

'Watch,' said the general as a door opened on the other side of the room.

In the sawdust circle, Paulo and Eliza turned to face the door as it opened. A man walked in. He was a

Quechua Indian and, just for an instant, Eliza thought her father had come back to help her. Her face lit up, then she saw that this man was much older than her father. His brown, high-cheekboned face was lined with age and his dark eyes watched her without emotion.

The man was holding the chains of two of the biggest dogs Paulo had ever seen. They stood as tall as Eliza on their huge, spreading paws. Their shoulders were powerful and muscled and their heads were twice the size of a man's. They were covered in short, honey-coloured hair, apart from a black muzzle and black, floppy triangular ears. The skin drooped above and beneath their dark eyes, giving them a sad expression, and the folds of their muzzles flapped loosely as they trotted over to investigate Paulo and Eliza.

Paulo stumbled back against the glass wall as the huge dogs came towards them. He pushed Eliza behind his back, trying to shield her, but the dogs merely shouldered him out of the way. One reared up and planted its front paws on his shoulders. He staggered under the enormous weight of the animal and would have fallen if it had not been for the glass wall at his back. The dog opened its mouth, showing a set of curved white teeth. Then its pink tongue flopped out and licked his face. It felt like being washed with a very large, very soft flannel.

Eliza was being washed too, but the other dog did not have to rear up to reach her face. She giggled with relief that the huge animal was friendly. The Quechua Indian stood impassively until the general flicked a switch on an intercom on the other side of the glass.

'Proceed,' he said, his voice ringing out over the loudspeakers. The Quechua nodded, then he pulled the two dogs over to the other side of the room and secured their chains to two of a row of steel rings embedded in the concrete wall.

'These are two of my pets,' explained the general. 'I have ten of them in total. They are bull mastiffs – the heaviest dog breed on the planet. They weigh more than a fully-grown man, ninety kilos on average. The Romans trained them as warrior dogs and they were used to hunt down bears in the Middle Ages. They can outrun a man and snap a thigh bone in their mouths as easily as we might snap a matchstick. Their jaws can exert a pressure of two hundred kilos per square inch.'

In the sawdust circle, the Quechua Indian finished securing the dogs and walked over to Paulo as the general was talking. He took a thick, hinged steel bracelet from his pocket and clipped it around Paulo's wrist. Paulo stared at it, trying to understand what it was. It fitted far too snugly for him to slip it off over his hand, and there seemed to be no catch to release it, only a slot where a key might fit. It was heavy and well-made and the hinge was virtually invisible when it was closed. The key slot was set into a thicker section of the bracelet, which also had a dark glass bubble embedded in it.

Paulo looked over to Eliza. The Quechua was busy testing a bracelet on her skinny wrist, but he soon realized that it would simply slip off over her hand, so he squatted to attach it to her ankle instead.

'What are these for?' demanded Paulo, turning to face the general.

'You will find out soon,' said the general, pulling

a small metal box from his pocket and extending the aerial. He switched to Spanish for the next part of his speech, so that both Paulo and Eliza could understand what he was saying. Behind the screen, Alex, Li and Hex looked to Amber for a translation, but she shook her head in confusion as she struggled to keep up with what the general was saying.

'You see, mastiffs are not naturally aggressive, as my two pets have just demonstrated. They have to be trained to hunt, to attack. My dog-handler and I have trained these dogs to attack by teaching them to associate a particular noise with a great deal of pain. For months they wore special collars, which gave them strong electric shocks every time they heard this noise and now . . . Now they will hunt down and attack the source of that noise without mercy. When I flick the switch on this box here, your bracelets will make that noise. It is too high for the human ear to register, but you will know when your bracelets are active because a red light will flash inside the glass bubble. And, of course—' the general laughed – 'the dogs will attack you without mercy.'

Inside the circle, the Quechua Indian had just

finished attaching the bracelet to Eliza's ankle, when she reached out and laid a trembling hand on the top of his head. He looked up into her eyes with a startled expression.

'Help me, Grandfather,' she said in Quechua. The man was not really her grandfather – she was simply using the name all Quechua children used for older men, as a sign of respect.

A spasm of emotion crossed the Quechua man's face like a ripple in a pond. He reached up and gave her hand a squeeze, then he stood up. 'I cannot help you, little one,' he replied gently. Then he turned and left the training room, closing the door softly behind him. Paulo and Eliza backed up against the glass screen, watching the dogs warily.

Behind the screen the general reached for the switch on the box, just as Amber worked out what it was he had been saying. Her hand flew to her mouth and her eyes widened. 'Don't!' she cried, but she was too late. He had already flicked the switch.

An instant later, the two dogs in the training circle turned into snarling monsters.

Seventeen

The dogs lunged for Paulo and Eliza, pushing off with their powerful haunches and rearing into the air. The chains brought them up short when they were centimetres away. Eliza screamed and curled up in a ball in the sawdust. Paulo squashed himself against the glass as one of the dogs snapped at the air in front of his face. The whites of its eyes were red with fury and strings of thick spittle flew from its snarling muzzle. Again and again the maddened dogs lunged to the limit of their chains, until Paulo thought the rings would surely be pulled away from the wall. Then, suddenly, the huge animals stopped and retreated to the far wall, panting and whining and looking around them in bewilderment.

Paulo looked down at his bracelet and saw that the red light had stopped flashing inside the glass bubble. The Quechua Indian returned, stony-faced, and led the dogs from the room. Paulo sagged against the glass and a silence fell over the training circle.

'Magnificent, weren't they?' said the general softly. He straightened and clapped his hands together. 'And now, it is time for the hunt!'

The thin-faced man stepped forward and pulled four more steel bracelets from his pockets. Amber, Hex, Alex and Li struggled as hard as they could, but a few minutes later they were each wearing one of the bracelets and their handcuffs had been removed. The thin-faced man opened a door in the glass wall and pushed them through into the training circle. Li ran to Paulo and hugged him hard. He winced at the pain but encircled her in his arms and hugged her back.

'So touching,' said the general through the inter-com. 'Now, this will be interesting. I have never hunted more than two at once before, and there are six of you. Of course, one of you is small and one is – shall we say? – not in the best of health, so that will slow you down, but even so I think I shall be using all ten dogs today. Will loyalty keep you together? Or will you split up? I wonder. That way some of you might have a chance. Although I must tell you that no-one has managed to escape the dogs so far.'

The general rubbed his hands, observing them through the glass as though they were a particularly pleasing species of animal. They glowered back at him silently. 'Nothing to say?' said the general. 'No pleading for your lives? Yes, this will be interesting! We are right in the middle of my land here. The grounds stretch for many miles all around. There are no rules. You can choose to go where you like. I should tell you that you will not be able to remove or break the bracelets. They are too strong. You will not be able to muffle the sound, whatever you do. The dogs can pick this sound up even when the bracelet is held underwater. Of course, you are welcome to waste your time trying all these things, but if I were you, I would use your time to get as far away from the dogs as possible. You have a twenty-minute start, then I will activate the bracelets and let the dogs loose. Good luck.'

The general turned on his heel and left the building, followed by the thin-faced man. A few seconds later a pair of large double doors on the far side of the training circle swung silently open and sunshine flooded into the dark room.

'Quick!' gasped Amber, heading for the doors. 'We have to start running!'

'Wait a minute, Amber,' called Alex, stripping off his fleece jacket. 'We can't just dash off without a plan. We'd never make it.'

Amber turned back, near to panic. 'What? What do we do?'

'First, we need to strip off some of these clothes. We'll be far too hot otherwise.'

Amber, Li and Hex began stripping off their outer layers. Alex threw his waterproof jacket and trousers over to Paulo, followed by his knife. 'Do you think you can make some sort of a sling out of that, Paulo, so Hex and I can take turns at carrying Eliza on our backs?'

Paulo nodded and got to work.

'Aren't we even going to try getting these bracelets off?' asked Li.

Hex shook his head as he struggled out of his waterproof trousers. 'I think the general was telling the truth. They look pretty unbreakable to me.'

'I agree,' said Paulo.

'Whatever we do,' said Amber, 'I think we should stay together. That way we have more of a chance against the dogs when they catch up.'

Alex nodded absently. He was looking at the compass which was still hanging around Amber's neck. 'There is one way we have a chance to get out of this,' he said slowly.

'How?' asked Li.

'I saw a road when we came in on the plane. It runs from west to east along the northern boundary of the estate. If we use Amber's compass to keep us heading north – and if we run as hard as we can through whatever is in our way, we might just make it to the road before the dogs catch up. Then we can stop a car.'

'And what if there isn't a car?' asked Li.

'Do you have a better plan, Li?' retorted Hex.

'Here,' said Paulo, holding out an improvised, papoose-style carrier. 'It is done.'

'I'll take her first,' said Hex.

He brought the straps down over his shoulders and tied them to the straps coming around his waist, then Paulo gently lifted Eliza up and slipped her into the papoose.

'Which way, Amber?' asked Li.

Amber checked her compass, then pointed out of the doorway. 'That way, towards the forest,' she said.

'Will you be OK, Paulo?' asked Hex.

Paulo drew himself up and nodded determinedly. 'They are only bruises,' he said.

'Let's go then,' said Alex.

They raced out of the double doors and across the manicured circle of grass that surrounded the converted hut. There was no other building in sight and the area was totally deserted. The general was nowhere to be seen. Strangely, they found that more frightening than if he had been standing there waiting to see which way they went. He must have a lot of faith in the abilities of his dogs to let his intended prey wander off wherever it wanted to go.

'Remember,' panted Alex, 'we keep going north as straight as an arrow, through whatever we find in front of us. It's our only chance.'

They moved across the open space in a tight bunch, feeling very exposed in the bright sunshine. The grass gave way to a field full of corn and they crashed their way through the tall plants, ignoring the slicing cuts from the sharp-edged leaves.

'Five minutes gone,' panted Li, checking her watch when they emerged on the other side of the field.

They pounded on through a sloping meadow until they reached a lake. Alex launched himself from the bank into the murky green water without hesitation and began swimming strongly towards the other side. Amber and Li swam on either side of Paulo, ready to help him if his battered muscles gave out. Hex brought up the rear, swimming more slowly, with Eliza bobbing wide-eyed above his head and clutching at the back of his neck.

The slope was muddy on the other side, churned up by cattle coming down to drink. They crawled out onto the bank and clambered to their feet, covered in slime and mud and blood. Alex took over the task of carrying Eliza from a badly winded Hex and they struggled on, up the steepening slope.

'Twelve minutes gone,' gasped Li.

They had just reached the edge of the forest at the top of the long slope when Hex looked down at his bracelet and saw with a sinking heart that the red light had started to flash. Wordlessly he held his arm out to show the others. A second later they heard a deep, disturbing baying drifting across to them on the still air. They looked back and saw ten pale shapes burst from the training hut, followed by a man on a horse. The ten shapes arrowed straight towards them.

'Come on!' yelled Alex urgently.

They crashed into the forest, finding a fresh burst of speed from somewhere. The trees were well spaced, but there were many overhanging branches and tree roots to trip them up. They ran on as fast as they could, with Amber checking her compass and leading the way. Thorns snagged at their clothes and ripped their skin, adding to the cuts they had received in the cornfield. The slope of the ground grew steeper until they were virtually dragging themselves upwards, clinging onto tree roots and branches. And all the while, the maddened baying of the dogs grew louder and louder.

'How much further?' gasped Paulo, clutching at his side.

'Just keep running!' shouted Hex.

Suddenly a crashing sounded in the forest behind them. The dogs had reached the tree line.

Desperately, they pounded on as the baying behind them grew to an almost deafening level.

'I can see them!' shrieked Li. 'They're nearly on us!'

'It's lighter up ahead,' gasped Paulo.

He was right. The trees were thinning out. They crashed on through the undergrowth and suddenly the road appeared ahead of them through the trees. They tumbled out onto it and looked around them. It was little more than an unmade track, and it was deserted.

Paulo bent over, trying to catch his breath. Amber and Li clung together, sobbing. Alex untied the straps on the papoose and lowered Eliza to the ground. She jumped up and hurried over to Paulo. Hex found two stout branches and handed one to Alex. Their plan had failed, but they were not going to die without a fight. They could see the dogs now. Huge, pale shapes crashing through the trees with their red eyes glowing.

Then an open-topped off-roader careered around the corner and screeched to a halt beside them. The Quechua Indian jumped out, leaving the engine running. He grabbed Eliza and threw her up into the back of the vehicle, motioning to the others to climb up after her. As they scrambled in, the man slipped a chain from around his neck and grasped Eliza's ankle. There was a small key hanging from the chain and he deftly slotted it into the lock on her bracelet. The steel hinge sprang open and he pulled the bracelet from her leg.

'There, little one,' he said in Quechua.

'They're here!' yelled Alex as the huge mastiffs launched themselves from the forest onto the road.

The Quechua threw the key at Amber, then ran for the driver's seat, still clutching Eliza's bracelet. He never made it. Three of the dogs grabbed him by the arms and throat, bringing him crashing to the ground and the others piled in, snarling and tearing at him. The man began to scream, then the screams died into a wet, gurgling noise as his throat was ripped out. Paulo grabbed Eliza and turned her face to his chest so that she would not see what was happening to her friend.

'Do something!' begged Li.

Alex and Hex leaned over the side of the truck and began beating at the pack with the branches they had picked up. The maddened dogs ignored them.

General Manteca urged his horse out of the trees onto the road. He took in the situation with one glance, then reached into his pocket and pulled out the little metal box. He flicked the switch and the red flashing lights on their bracelets blinked out. The dogs stopped snarling and pulled away from the body of the Quechua Indian. Some of them wandered about on the road as though they weren't quite sure how they got there, while others nudged at the tattered remains of their master and whined softly.

The general looked down at the body of his dog-trainer, then turned his cold eyes on the five of them where they huddled together in the back of the off-roader. He got down from his horse and tied the reins to a tree, then he pulled a high-powered rifle from the saddle bag and took aim at the back of the off-roader, trying to decide who to shoot first.

Alex bowed his head and waited for the bullets to hit. They never came. Suddenly, half a dozen men in camouflage gear materialized out of the trees, with their weapons trained on the general. One of the men was his father. Alex grinned as a huge wave of astonished relief swept over him.

'Lower your rifle, Luis,' instructed Alex's father in a cold voice.

The general stared in shock at the six men surrounding him, then glanced towards the trees, judging his chances.

'You won't make it,' Alex's father went on, in the same cold voice.

The general slowly lowered his rifle, then laid it on the ground. Two of the men hurried forward and collected the rifle, then frisked the general. Alex recognized one of the men as Mike. They removed the little metal box and a cellphone from his pockets, then stepped back.

Alex's father hurried over to the off-roader and Alex opened his mouth to speak, but his father only glanced without recognition at the group of mud-, slime- and blood-covered kids in the back before reaching in and turning off the ignition. '*No se mueva*,' he ordered, before turning all his attention back to the general. *He thinks we're street kids*, thought Alex, watching his father in open fascination. He was seeing a completely different side of him. A side that had always been off-limits to Alex.

'When did you get back?' asked the general, as though he had merely bumped into Alex's father in the street.

'Last night. Guayaquil was a dead-end, but of course you knew that.'

'How did you find out . . .?'

'About you? A street kid came and found me. Leo, he was called.'

In the back of the off-roader, Amber raised her eyes to the sky. Leo! She had forgotten all about him. She sent a silent thank-you to Leo for doing as she had asked.

'Leo?' The general shook his head. 'Don't know him.'

'No, of course you don't,' said Alex's dad. 'The only street kids you know are dead ones. Leo knew you, though. He told me all about you.'

'And how did you find this place?' asked the general.

'That was easy,' said Alex's dad, holding up the cellphone that Mike had passed to him. 'I sent a text message from Paris this morning.'

'Ah,' smiled the general. 'Very clever. Then you pinpointed the location of the signal.'

'We were in the woods, moving in to reconnoitre the house, when all hell broke loose.'

'A man has to have some hobbies,' said the general. 'I always love to hunt on a beautiful day like this.'

'You won't be doing any more hunting today. I'm taking you back to Quito to face charges of murder and the manufacture and smuggling of cocaine.'

'You can try, my friend, but it won't work. You can't do anything to me in my own country. I am too powerful here. Too many people owe me a favour.'

'I thought you might say that,' said Alex's dad. He

turned to the off-roader and looked at Amber, who was still clutching the key to the bracelets. 'Take off the rest of the bracelets,' he instructed her in Spanish. 'Then throw them over here, with the key.'

Amber hurried to carry out the instructions as Alex's dad turned back to the general. She started with Alex. Once the bracelet was off, Alex's eyes widened as he spotted the tell-tale ring of white skin that had been revealed beneath. No street kid had skin that pale. Quickly Alex hid his hand behind his back, but his father had not noticed. He was busy with the general.

'You have two choices, Luis,' said Alex's father. He held up his cellphone. 'One: you can call the Justice Department and all the national newspapers right now, stating who you are and making a full confession.'

The general laughed. 'And the second choice?' he asked.

Alex's father picked up the bracelets from the ground where Amber had thrown them. Then he bent and retrieved the final bracelet from the hand of the Quechua Indian. He linked all the bracelets together, leaving the one at the end of the chain open. He stepped forward and clipped this final bracelet around the general's wrist.

'The second choice,' he said, holding up the little metal box, 'is to take your chances with the dogs.'

There was a long silence as the two men stared at one another. Finally Alex's father spoke again. 'Do any of you kids drive?' he called in Spanish, without turning his head away from the general.

'I do,' replied Paulo.

'Then get out of here,' ordered Alex's dad. 'All of you.'

Paulo clambered over the seats, hanging onto the roll bars of the off-roader, and settled himself in the driver's seat. Eliza scrambled after him, her eyes big with panic in case he was planning to leave her. She pressed herself against his side and Paulo smiled down at her reassuringly. Quickly he checked the controls. They were pretty much the same as the off-roaders he was used to driving on his ranch. Paulo started the engine and put the off-roader into gear. He hesitated, looking over at the SAS men.

'Go!' ordered Alex's dad.

Paulo hit the accelerator and the off-roader took off down the track in a cloud of dust. Alex stared back at the silent group of men standing by the track until they disappeared from view.

A few minutes later they all heard the dreadful baying of the dogs start up again.

The general had made his choice.

Amber shuddered and moved closer to Hex in the back of the off-roader. He put an arm around her shoulders.

'That was close,' said Li, in a shaken voice. 'We were nearly finished.'

'Remind me to thank Leo next time I see him,' said Hex.

'That was my dad, you know,' said Alex proudly.

'We guessed that,' said Amber.

'He didn't even recognize me.'

'That doesn't surprise me,' said Amber. 'Have you looked in a mirror lately?'

Alex leaned forward and stared into the rear-view mirror. His face and hair were completely caked in drying mud and green weed. He grinned at the sight and his teeth shone brightly against the dirt.

'Where to?' asked Paulo from the front seat.

'Are you OK to drive?' asked Alex.

Paulo nodded. 'I am fine. Just bruised.'

'Then let's head back to Quito,' said Alex

'OK,' said Paulo, 'but you had better settle down now and put on your seatbelts. I do not have a licence, so we must not draw attention to ourselves.'

Alex, Li, Hex and Amber looked at one another in the back seat. They were all dressed in thermal longjohns and plastered with mud.

'Oh, yeah, that'll do it,' spluttered Amber. 'Once we put our seatbelts on, we won't stand out at all!'

They all collapsed in the back seat. All the tension of the last few days poured out in wild, hysterical hoots of laughter. Paulo tried to frown seriously, but soon he was laughing too. The laughter was infectious and even little Eliza joined in, even though she had no idea what the joke was.

The off-roader reached the end of the track, turned onto the busy Pan-American Highway and headed for Quito, trailing hoots of laughter behind it all the way.

EIGHTEEN

Sister Catherine's House was a large old building in
the heart of the Old Town. The paint was peeling
and the plaster was crumbling, but the big double
doors to the courtyard were open wide and a warm
light was shining out onto the cobbled street.

The five members of Alpha Force climbed out of
the taxi and stared up at the old house. Paulo reached
back in to help Eliza out onto the street while Amber
paid the taxi-driver. They all looked a lot better than
they had two days earlier. The swelling around
Paulo's eye had nearly gone, although the bruising
was now a spectacular combination of green and
purple. The doctor Amber's uncle brought to the
hotel had given them all a thorough physical and
declared them fit and well. He had given Paulo pain-

killers and anti-inflammatories, and he had treated Eliza for worms and lice.

For two days they had lain low in the hotel, eating, resting and getting their strength back. Now it was Christmas Eve and they had a plane to catch. Amber's uncle had flown back to New York earlier that day. Alpha Force were flying out to Argentina later that night to spend Christmas together on Paulo's ranch, but first they had one final task to complete.

Alex took a hasty look up and down the street before he stepped into the circle of light coming from the courtyard. He knew his father was still out at the general's estate and would be there for the next few days, gathering the information to convict as many members of the drug-smuggling ring as he could, but Alex was still a little nervous, half-expecting his father to come striding around the next corner.

Eliza held back, staring up at the big house apprehensively, so Paulo scooped her up on one arm and picked up her overnight bag with the other. Eliza looked completely different. Her hair shone, her cheeks had a healthy glow and the sores and scabs on her skin were healing fast. The only thing that had not changed was the sad look in her eyes. Paulo looked at her little face and felt his heart twist. It was going to be hard to leave Eliza here, but he knew it had to be done.

They walked through the double doors into the courtyard and stopped in astonishment. A huge party was going on under the stars. The bushes were festooned with lanterns and a long row of tables had been set against the end wall. They were piled high with the food that all Quito families ate together on Christmas Eve. There were huge stuffed turkeys, bowls of grapes and raisins, massive platters of rice and cheese and piles of steaming sweetcorn. Tureens of hot chocolate and baskets filled with cookies stood on the end table. Street kids swarmed everywhere, filling their plates or chasing one another in and out of the courtyard arches. Some of them were adding Christmas party hats to the traditional Quito life-sized Nativity scene in the corner, helped by a plump young woman dressed in jeans and a T-shirt.

Paulo took Eliza off to the tables of food, while

the other four made their way over to the young woman. Amber cleared her throat and tried out her best Spanish. 'Excuse me,' she said. 'We are looking for Sister Catherine.'

The young woman turned to face them. Her face was flushed and her eyes sparkled. 'It's OK,' she said. 'You can speak English.'

Amber grinned with relief. 'Phew! My Spanish isn't that good. Quite a party you have going on here.'

'Yeah, well, we have a lot to celebrate,' said the young woman. 'The spirit of Christmas is alive and well in Quito! Can you believe an anonymous donor has given us millions – and I mean *millions* – of dollars?' She hugged herself with excitement. 'I still can't quite take it in. We have such plans! More houses, of course, and schools, and—' The young woman stopped and smiled at them. 'But you don't want to hear all that. How can I help you?'

'We're looking for Sister Catherine,' said Li.

'You've found her,' said the young woman.

'You're Sister Catherine?' Alex gaped openly before he remembered his manners.

Sister Catherine laughed. 'Not all nuns wear

habits and drift about looking holy, you know! So, how can I help?'

Amber's face grew serious. 'We have someone we want you to look after,' she said, pointing out Eliza, who was still clinging to Paulo. 'Her name is Eliza. She's been through a lot. Her parents and her older brother are dead. She left her younger brother Toby here for adoption eight months ago, so she's all on her own.'

Sister Catherine nodded understandingly. 'Eliza will be welcome here. And, now we have all this money, we can offer her great things! Health and education. Perhaps even a place at university if she chooses. Great things!'

'The thing is,' said Li, 'I think there might be a scene when we try to leave her. She's become very attached to Paulo.'

Sister Catherine smiled. 'I think I know what to do about that. The best thing a person can do when they are feeling small and lonely is to take care of someone else. I will bring one of the younger boys down and ask Eliza to take care of him. Then she will have a reason to stay. Wait here.'

Sister Catherine hurried off and the four of them were left standing in the middle of the courtyard. Amber looked around and spotted a familiar figure lurking in the shadows beyond the arches. He was stuffing turkey into his mouth and glaring around as though someone might try to steal it from him. Amber grinned broadly. 'Leo!' she yelled, waving madly.

Leo jumped, then glared out at her for a few seconds before slipping away.

'*Gracias*, Leo! *Gracias*!' called Amber after his retreating back. Leo flinched as though she had hit him.

'Here we are!' said Sister Catherine, behind them. They turned to see her holding the hand of a little boy of three. He was in his pyjamas and was still rubbing the sleep from his eyes.

'Hello,' said Li, smiling down at the little boy and holding out her hand.

He glared up at her, then, quick as a snake, tried to bite her hand. Li snatched it away just in time.

'He does that a lot,' said Sister Catherine calmly. 'Mainly to people he thinks are going to try to adopt him.'

'I'm not sure this is going to work,' said Alex, looking from the ferocious little boy to Eliza, who was still clinging to Paulo's neck.

'Oh, it will work,' said Sister Catherine. 'This is a very special little boy. Watch.'

She turned and called across the courtyard. 'Eliza!'

Eliza turned in Paulo's arms and looked at Sister Catherine, who pointed down at the little boy. Eliza followed the pointing finger, then her eyes widened in delighted astonishment. She jumped out of Paulo's arms and ran across the courtyard. The little boy spotted her and gave a wordless cry, full of yearning and relief. Eliza grabbed the little boy up in her arms and held him tight as he burst into noisy tears. Eliza pushed the blond curls away from his face and wiped his eyes with her sleeve, talking to him softly in Quechua. The tears were flowing down her own face, but she did not seem to notice.

'Toby,' said Amber wonderingly. 'This is Toby?'

'Yes,' smiled Sister Catherine.

'But Eliza was sure he would be adopted quickly,' said Paulo, coming up behind them. 'Because of his blond hair.'

'Oh, he could have been adopted twenty times over,' said Sister Catherine, 'but he kept biting them. Said he wasn't leaving because his sister Eliza would be back for him. Seems he was right.'

Eliza led Toby over to the tables of food and started picking out the tastiest morsels for him. He followed, clinging to her skirt and looking up at her as though she might vanish again at any minute.

'Happy endings,' said Amber, her voice full of tears. 'Don'tcha just love 'em?'

She looked over to Sister Catherine and saw Leo lurking just behind her. Sister Catherine continued to smile over at Eliza and Toby, but her hand whipped behind her and caught Leo's hand in a grip of iron, just as he was sliding her wallet out of the back pocket of her jeans. She twisted her hand, still smiling at Eliza and Toby, and Leo bent over behind her, his face a silent picture of pain.

Leo had just met his match.

'Sometimes,' said Sister Catherine pleasantly, 'I put a mousetrap in there. So watch out.'

She let go of Leo's hand, still not looking round at

him. Leo slunk away into the shadows, rubbing his crushed fingers.

'You sorted him out!' grinned Hex, but Sister Catherine's face was sad as she looked at him.

'That one, he's been on the streets too long. We can hope, but it may be too late for him.' She looked back at Eliza and Toby and her face brightened again. 'But those two, now that's a completely different story.'

'I think,' said Paulo, 'it would be better to just slip away.'

Sister Catherine nodded. 'Merry Christmas,' she called softly, as Alpha Force headed for the door.

They stepped out onto the cobbled street and walked away from Sister Catherine's House, each wrapped in their own thoughts. It had been quite a week. There had been a lot of deaths and a lot of danger. They were all feeling sad to be leaving Eliza but happy to have successfully completed their first mission. The night sky was clear and full of stars. Alex looked up, just as the first of a series of huge fireworks exploded over the Old Town of Quito.

'Merry Christmas, Alpha Force,' said Alex, beginning to smile.

'Merry Christmas!' replied Li, Paulo, Hex and Amber, smiling too.

The five members of Alpha Force moved closer together in the quiet street, content just to watch for a while as giant streamers of colour fizzed across the night sky above them.

CHRIS RYAN'S TOP TEN TIPS FOR SURVIVAL IN MOUNTAIN CONDITIONS

If you're stuck on a mountain, whether it has forested slopes or is covered in snow and ice, it will almost certainly be high, inhospitable, difficult to travel across – and it will be hard to find someone lost there. The sheer scale of the surrounding terrain may make you feel that survival is impossible. It's NOT– not if you keep your head and make use of any survival skills you have.

1. PREPARATION IS THE FIRST ESSENTIAL

If you are heading off into mountain regions, make sure you tell the relevant authorities – like the police or mountain rescue – where you are going and how long you plan to be gone. If there is a disaster, rescue attempts will be made sooner and it will be easier for them to find you. Certain basic equipment is also advisable:

MY BASIC SURVIVAL KIT CONTAINS
- ropes
- a small shovel or other digging equipment
- a sleeping bag or poncho or large waterproof sheet for shelter if necessary
- a knife
- waterproof matches
- medical equipment including: painkillers (broken limbs are possible in mountainous conditions), plasters or butterfly sutures for wounds, antiseptic
- sun goggles if going into a snowy area, to protect your eyes
- tea bags and stock cubes to make hot drinks
- mini-flares for signalling
- vitamin pills
- thermal and waterproof clothing

2. STAY CALM AND STAY PUT

If you have told the authorities where you plan to be going, it's a good idea to stay close to your planned route to help any rescue efforts, finding the best nearby place to shelter. You can then use your energy for survival until rescue, rather than just heading off blindly into what could be a worse situation.

The higher you go, the thinner the air is too, so you will probably find yourself getting tired more easily and suffering the first signs of altitude sickness: breathlessness, a fast pulse, headaches and dizziness. Conserve your energy, don't panic and try and work out what your best course of action is to be.

If you must move . . .

3. PUT SAFETY BEFORE SPEED

Mountain slopes can be very slippery – especially slopes covered with scree, or loose rocks, and you don't want to risk a fall. Snow can cover up deep crevasses, so move very carefully, testing the ground ahead of you with a stick before taking a step. If going downhill, go backwards, using your heels and a stick as a brake. If going uphill, climb in a zig-zag, using a stick for extra support. Believe me, tobogganing down a snowy mountain without a toboggan is not a good idea! Once, when I first joined the regiment, we were climbing in the Alps and two good friends fell to their deaths because they lost their footing, so it is important to take your time when descending from a mountain.

If you're in a group, and the ground is very treacherous, try roping yourselves together with about 10 metres between each of you and move very slowly indeed. Travel only in daylight when you can see where you are going.

4. FIND SHELTER

This is essential in any cold conditions to maintain body temperature. If you start feeling confused or shivery, stumble more than you should and find it hard to get your body to do what you want, you could be showing the first signs of what is known as hypothermia – when your body temperature drops faster than your body can generate heat.

Hypothermia can kill you! If you've ever got soaked on a cold, wet day, you'll know how miserable you can feel and, believe me, it only gets worse if you are out in these conditions for a long period of time. Hypothermia, which is no joke, is something I have suffered from and watched two friends die from it. Remember, though, that if you lose heat slowly, you also need to warm up bit by bit, rather than all at once. Try to get out of the wind and into shelter, create a source of heat, eat or drink something warm and replace wet clothes with dry (one piece at a time – don't strip everything off at once). Huddling together can also help: it's amazing how much heat another body can provide.

A small cave would make an ideal shelter (as long as nothing's living in it already!), or you could shelter underneath an overhanging rock. If there are trees around, the branches can be pulled down to create a windbreak and in deep snowy conditions, you can dig underneath the branches of trees to create a hollow protected by the tree.

If there is nothing but snow in sight, pile up snow to make a windbreak or dig out a trench, piling the snow up the windiest side. Remember, though, that if you make something out of snow, keep any digging tools with you inside in case you have to dig yourself out again! Also, do think about ventilation. In Norway, I remember being in a snow hole, the hole was blocked and we started to fall asleep. Luckily, one of the team woke, realized we were suffering from carbon monoxide poisoning and kicked a hole in the roof to get fresh air in.

5. LIGHT A FIRE

A fire will provide heat – and it will cheer you up! You can also heat up food and drink and dry your clothes by it. If you have found shelter in a cave, build the fire as high as possible at the back so that the hot air rises. If you build it at the front, it might fill the cave with smoke so you can't breathe.

6. WATER

Water is always a survival essential. Look for a fresh water supply – at the bottom of a valley is a good place – or leave containers to catch rainwater. In snowy conditions, use a fire to melt ice (ice melts quicker than snow). If you're on the move or don't have a fire, you will still need to replace fluids somehow. Don't eat snow – it will just settle in your stomach as a cold lump and make you colder from the inside out. In an emergency, form the snow into snowballs and hold one in your mouth, allowing it to melt slowly.

7. EAT SOMETHING

Food is another priority if you are likely to be stuck for a long period. Your body needs more food in low temperatures, too. In a group, ration any supplies so that it will last as long as possible.

Vegetation is usually pretty thin on the ground in mountain areas, but birds and their eggs can be a good source of food. Follow their droppings to see where they nest, but take care – a flock of angry gulls protecting their eggs can be vicious. Crawl as close as you can and try and take eggs only if the birds are not present. You might also be able to knock down a bird with stones or sticks, or make a trap to catch them. Once, in a survival situation, I caught some seagulls. These birds didn't taste too good as they are scavengers and will eat anything!

8. WATCH THE WEATHER

Unless you like the idea of being buried under a heap of snow, watch out for the possibility of an avalanche. Try not to make your shelter under smooth, steep snow slopes – a more rugged landscape is less likely to suddenly come loose and land on your head and avoid shouting as this can set the snow off. Finally, if the worst does come to the worst and a heap of snow roars down towards you, try and 'swim' on top of it rather than fighting it. Before setting out, listen to the local radio station for any avalanche warnings. If there is a high risk of one, it would be advisable to wear an avalanche transmitter. If you happen to be buried, this sends out a signal so that the rescue team can then locate you.

9. TREAT ANY INJURIES

It's easy to trip over a rock or put your foot down a hole and broken limbs are a definite possibility in any accident. Immobilise a broken or sprained limb with a splint made out of a straight stick and treat any cuts with antiseptic cream or powder. If you're stuck without supplies, one tip is that you can use your urine to wash out a wound (don't do this without telling the injured person first though – they might take it the wrong way!).

As well as hypothermia, there are several other different health problems that could affect you in cold, mountainous areas. Everyone knows that polar explorers suffer from frostbite but you don't need arctic conditions to get it; vulnerable places like your face, nose, ears, hands and feet can get frostbite if exposed to temperatures of $-1°C$ for long periods (and that can easily happen in cold, windy areas). Watch out for feelings of prickliness, then numb, waxy-looking patches. If you do get it, you will need to thaw out the affected skin slowly, using warm water rather than direct heat from a fire. You could also try the old trick of putting your feet on someone else's stomach (tell them first!).

In snow, snow blindness can also be a problem as the glare of the sun reflects back off the snow. This can happen in as little as fifteen minutes. If you start blinking and squinting to see, then begin seeing everything in a nice rosy glow, you're in trouble. Cover your eyes – blindfold them if necessary – or you could risk being temporarily blinded. Wearing goggles protects your eyes from this risk and you could also try rubbing charcoal underneath your eyes to reduce the glare.

As the ultraviolet light of the sun reflects off snow, you can also get bad sunburn on any unprotected skin. This includes areas like the inside of your nose!

10. SIGNAL FOR RESCUE

This is going to be a big priority, especially if no-one knows where you are. A fire will produce smoke and attract attention but it's also a good idea to lay out some ground-to-air signals. This can be as simple as laying out stones in a pattern to spell out SOS – or tramping snow down to make these letters. Make it as big as you can so it's easily visible from the air.

If you spot a rescue helicopter or plane, there are some internationally recognized signals which all mountain rescue teams understand, using flares, a whistle or flashes of light from a torch. The most important to know is the one for SOS – a request for help.

SOS

Flare: red

Sound: three short blasts, three long, three short
(repeat after a 1-minute interval)

Light: 6 flashes in quick succession (repeat after a
1-minute interval)

BE SAFE!

Chris Ryan

Random House Children's Books and Chris Ryan would like to make it clear that these tips are for use in a serious situation only, where your life may be at risk. We cannot accept any liability for inappropriate usage in normal conditions.

About the Author

Chris Ryan joined the SAS in 1984 and has been involved in numerous operations with the regiment. During the Gulf War, he was the only member of an eight-man team to escape from Iraq, three colleagues being killed and four captured. It was the longest escape and evasion in the history of the SAS. For this he was awarded the Military Medal. He wrote about his remarkable escape in the adult bestseller *The One That Got Away* (1995), which was also adapted for screen.

He left the SAS in 1994 and is now the author of a number of bestselling thrillers for adults. His work in security takes him around the world and he has also appeared in a number of television series, most recently *Hunting Chris Ryan*, in which his escape and evasion skills were demonstrated to the max. The *Alpha Force* titles are his first books for young readers.

If you enjoyed this book, you might like to read
the first Alpha Force adventure:

ALPHA FORCE

Mission: Survival

SURVIVAL

Alex, Li, Paulo, Hex and Amber are five teenagers on
board a sailing ship crewed by young people from all
over the world. Together they are marooned on a desert
island. And together they must face the ultimate test –
survival! Battling against unbelievable dangers – from
killer komodo dragons to sharks and modern-day pirates
– the five must combine all their knowledge and skills if
they are to stay alive.

The team – Alpha Force – is born . . .

ISBN 0 099 43924 7

If you enjoyed this book look out for others in the series:

ALPHA FORCE

Target: Toxic Waste

HOSTAGE

Alpha Force are five teenagers who have formed a highly-skilled squad to help in the international fight against evil. Flying to Northern Canada to investigate reports of illegal dumping of toxic waste, the team must dive into an icy river, cross the harsh landscape on snowmobiles and mobilize their caving skills to complete their mission. But they need all their courage and determination when they come face-to-face with a man who is ready to kill – or take a hostage – to stop them.

The team face their toughest challenge yet . . .

ISBN 0 099 43927 1